SUNDAY

BLOODY

SUNDAY

PENELOPE GILLIATT

SUNDAY BLOODY SUNDAY

The Script of the John Schlesinger Film

Produced by Joseph Janni for United Artists

NEW YORK / THE VIKING PRESS

John Schlesinger and Joseph Janni worked through
the later versions of the screenplay with me and I
thank them, as well as the actors and the crew.

P.G.

THE PLAYERS

Alex Greville—GLENDA JACKSON
Dr. Daniel Hirsh—PETER FINCH
Bob Elkin—MURRAY HEAD
Mrs. Greville—PEGGY ASHCROFT
Mr. Greville—MAURICE DENHAM
Alva Hodson—VIVIAN PICKLES
Bill Hodson—FRANK WINDSOR
Professor Johns—THOMAS BAPTISTE
Mr. Harding (Businessman)—TONY BRITTON
Daniel's Father—HAROLD GOLDBLATT
Daniel's Mother—HANNAH NORBERT
Middle-aged Patient—RICHARD PEARSON
Woman Patient—JUNE BROWN
Rowing Woman (Daniel's Party)—CAROLINE BLAKISTON
Her Husband (Daniel's Party)—PETER HALLIDAY
Man at Daniel's Party—DOUGLAS LAMBERT
Answering Service Lady—BESSIE LOVE
Aunt Astrid—MARIE BURKE
Tony (Bob's Friend)—RICHARD LONCRAINE
Scotsman—JON FINCH
Alex as a Child—CINDY BURROWS
Lucy Hodson—KIMI TALLMADGE
Timothy Hodson—RUSSELL LEWIS
Tess Hodson—EMMA SCHLESINGER
Baby, John-Stuart Hodson—PATRICK THORNBERRY

THE FILM-MAKERS

Producer	JOSEPH JANNI
Director	JOHN SCHLESINGER
Associate Producer	TEDDY JOSEPH
Screenwriter	PENELOPE GILLIATT
Production Manager	HUGH HARLOW
Location Manager	LEE BOLON
1st Assistant Director	SIMON RELPH
Continuity	ANN SKINNER
Director of Photography	BILLY WILLIAMS
Camera Operator	DAVID HARCOURT
Production Designer	LUCIANA ARRIGHI
Costume Designer	JOCELYN RICKARDS
Art Director	NORMAN DORME
Editor	RICHARD MARDEN
Sound Mixer	SIMON KAYE
Chief Make-up Artist	FREDDY WILLIAMSON
Hairdressing	BETTY GLASOW

IN COLOR

UNITED ARTISTS, Entertainment from Transamerica Corporation

SUNDAY
BLOODY
SUNDAY

Black screen.

Title in white.

Voices over, continuing for a few seconds while screen stays black. A MIDDLE-AGED MAN PATIENT, earnestly hypochondriacal, and DR. DANIEL HIRSH.

FRIDAY

DANIEL

Tell me if you feel anything?

MAN PATIENT

No.

DANIEL

There?

MAN PATIENT

No.

DANIEL

There?

MAN PATIENT

No. I told you, it's over the other side.

DANIEL

There?

MAN PATIENT

No.

DANIEL

There?

FRIDAY

MAN PATIENT

Yes, that's it.

DANIEL

I can't feel anything.

MAN PATIENT

Yes. My appendix side.
(thoughtful wince)

Cut to DANIEL's hands on PATIENT's stomach.
Movements.

DANIEL

I think we're fine.

MAN PATIENT

What do you mean, we're fine?

DANIEL

I think we ought to lose a little weight.

MAN PATIENT

Why do doctors say "we"? As if it were *your* pain.

DANIEL
(begins to move to wash-basin)
Why don't you put your clothes on?

MAN PATIENT motionless.

PULL BACK ON DANIEL HIRSH'S CONSULT-
ING ROOM IN HIS HOUSE IN PEMBROKE
SQUARE. EVENING. FRIDAY, ABOUT 6:00 P.M.

The title "FRIDAY" appears on the film screen.

DANIEL is a doctor in his early forties. Jewish. Clever,
humorous face. He has a system of dispensing stoicism
that helps to keep at bay his own difficulties. His consulting room is part of his house, small and pleasant.

4

FRIDAY

Little jade elephants and ivory pigs on his desk. A silver photograph of his mother and father, playing two pianos and laughing, stands on a bookshelf behind him. A geodesic sculpture is visible through the window, set in a pretty walled garden with a rock pool.

> DANIEL
> *(washing his hands)*
> I think it's just possible you've got colitis. Mild colitis.

PATIENT goes on lying down. DANIEL begins to dry his hands.

> MAN PATIENT
> Colitis can be very serious.

> DANIEL
> Look, stop worrying, eh? It may be worry that's hurting you.

MAN PATIENT sulks. DANIEL moves from couch to desk, taking off his stethoscope.

> DANIEL
> I wish you'd stop reading the "Medical Journal."
> *(in motion, seen from back)*
> Remember the pain you had when you thought you had a brain tumour and it was your bowler hat?

> MAN PATIENT
> *(haughty, cut to the quick)*
> This *does* hurt.

> DANIEL
> Yes.
> *(pause)*
> I think perhaps it might be an idea if you went in for a few tests.

5

FRIDAY

MAN PATIENT
(looking over screen)
Tests! There's something critical.

DANIEL
There's *nothing* critical.
(affection. Firmness)
There's no question of that.
*(he means cancer, which he can see in the
PATIENT's mind)*
It's just in case there's colitis.

MAN PATIENT
You're hiding something from me.

DANIEL
I'm not hiding anything from you. This is probably
nothing at all—

The buzzer goes. DANIEL picks up the receiver and
speaks. The PATIENT stops dressing, stranded. He still
has his shoes to put on and stands there in his socks.

DANIEL
(to SECRETARY)
Ask him to give me a minute.
*(he puts his hand over the receiver and goes
on talking to the PATIENT)*
—But I've got to be sure, O.K.?
*(pause. Gaze between them. DANIEL takes his
hand off the receiver and speaks)*
Sorry. Look, I'm with a patient.

The MAN PATIENT sees an advantage to be had from
DANIEL's intimate voice.

MAN PATIENT
(silky)
Do you want me to leave?

DANIEL

No, of course not. Finish dressing and come over
here.
(into receiver)
Can I ring you back . . . ? Well, it shouldn't be
long, but I can't now. Try and stay in for a few
minutes, will you? . . . O.K., but just *stay there*
for a few minutes, can't you? Right . . .
(after putting receiver down)
Now, how's next week?

MAN PATIENT

I can't next week. I've got to go to Brussels.

DANIEL

All right, then. The one after.

MAN PATIENT
(scared, getting out diary)
I think I'm going to Frankfurt.

DANIEL

Look, which is more important, the pain or Frankfurt?

MAN PATIENT

I came to be examined. Can't you tell by examina-
tion, for heaven's sake?

DANIEL

Look, I'm not a fortune teller, you know. I'm only
a doctor.

The buzzer goes twice. The PATIENT looks up from his
diary.

MAN PATIENT

Again?

7

FRIDAY

DANIEL

It's only Ann to say she's going home. She's putting the telephone through.

MAN PATIENT

It'll be ringing in *here* all the time now.
(he really is rather rattled, and DANIEL *sees it)*

DANIEL

The answering service'll take it.

MAN PATIENT leans forward.

MAN PATIENT

I'd much rather you *told* me.

DANIEL

Listen, old friend. It's not cancer.

MAN PATIENT

How do you know?

DANIEL

I'm telling you.

The telephone goes. Three rings. It stops as the ANSWER-ING SERVICE picks up. Then DANIEL picks up and listens for a few minutes before he puts the receiver down, click.

MAN PATIENT

Someone you didn't want to speak to?

DANIEL

(standing and handing the prescription to the patient, grinning at him a bit)
German measles.

FRIDAY

THE OUTSIDE OF DANIEL'S HOUSE IN PEMBROKE SQUARE. EARLY EVENING.

London County Council rubbish van. Dustbin business. Potted bushes for sale are visible at the end of the square, promising a good summer. Through the folded tennis net in the middle of the square we see DANIEL opening the door and shaking the PATIENT's hand. PATIENT walks away.

DANIEL'S KITCHEN. EVENING.

DANIEL has just finished dialling on the telephone. We can hear the engaged sound. The receiver is on the side of his head that faces camera, obscuring a lot of his profile (a device used through the film whenever one of the characters fails to get through on a call).

DANIEL opens fridge door, finds a bar of chocolate, and starts to eat.

Detail of telephone exchange transmitting engaged number electronically.

DANIEL'S WAITING ROOM (IN PRIVATE LIFE, HIS DINING ROOM). EVENING.

Similar shot of DANIEL's head, hand, and receiver, against a wall of another colour. Engaged sound on track.

Pull back to show him in room. He puts down the receiver and starts to turn the waiting room back into his dining room—piling away copies of *Punch* and *Tatler* into the sideboard, moving candlesticks from the sideboard to the dining table. An ironically sublime section of "Così fan Tutte," used at moments through the film, comes in here.

DANIEL'S WAITING ROOM. EVENING.

DANIEL sits on the edge of a table, dialling the ANSWERING SERVICE.

9

FRIDAY

DANIEL

(on telephone)
It's Dr. Hirsh.

ANSWERING SERVICE

What was the name?

DANIEL

Dr. *Daniel* Hirsh. What were those calls?

ANSWERING SERVICE

I thought I heard you picking up.

DANIEL

Yes, but I didn't take the *numbers*. I had a patient.
(acid)
That's why I didn't speak to them, you see.

ANSWERING SERVICE

Well, there was a call from Dr. Simon; and a call
from Mrs. Burke, she says you have the number;
and from Mr. Elgin.

DANIEL

Yes. Did Mr. Elkin say how long he'd be in?

ANSWERING SERVICE

He said he was going out straight away.

DANIEL

Well, he must have changed his mind. He's still in
because it's engaged.

ANSWERING SERVICE

It might be somebody else ringing him.

DANIEL

Look, I do *know* it might be somebody else ringing him.
(dignity)
But he needs to speak to me urgently before he

goes away for the weekend, you see. Never mind. Next time, try to give me his name—

Shot of ANSWERING SERVICE face. Profile and machinery.

> DANIEL (voice over)
—roughly right, just this once? It adds a personal touch. Elkin, not Elgin, and not Alvin either, not Allcott, not Higgins. You've been taking it long enough, for Christ's sake—no, I'm going straight out now.

DANIEL'S WAITING ROOM. EVENING.

DANIEL moves chairs into their dining-table position and dials again on the telephone. It starts to ring.

DANIEL'S IMAGINATION, FILTER SHOT. BOB ELKIN'S STUDIO/PAD. SAME TIME. EARLY EVENING.

BOB is a Londoner of twenty-five who makes a living out of designing plastic furniture, kinetic sculpture and various bits of paraphernalia.

Telephone ringing. BOB going out, ignoring it, putting finger in his TOUCAN's beak. The bell goes on in the empty room. Clutter. Coke bottles, a garden swing-seat used as a sofa, a metal robot seated on a low shelf with work tools and cassettes beside it. Japanese paper lamps, a harmonograph, posters, old socks and sweaters and underclothes. An architect's desk piled with BOB's gadget-making in progress. The calmest thing in the room is the head of a long-horn buffalo on a white wall. The telephone stops. Silence in the room. The TOUCAN jumps up onto the window and looks out.

DANIEL'S IMAGINATION, FILTER SHOT. BOB'S PAD. EVENING.

BOB, sitting alone in his pad, close to the ringing telephone and not answering it. He lights a cigarette.

FRIDAY

Close-up of BOB full-face, smoking. (DANIEL's imagination, filter shot.) Ringing telephone sound over.

DANIEL'S CONSULTING ROOM. EVENING.

DANIEL, reaction shot, listening to the ringing sound.

BOB'S PAD. REALITY.

Same time. Totally static view, wide. Telephone ringing in the empty flat, shortly stopping. Then it rings again.

ALEX'S STUDIO. SAME TIME. EVENING.

ALEX is a bright, tender young woman of thirty-four, divorced a couple of years ago. She has a witty face and a habit of peering at people attentively when they talk. It is due slightly to short sight but mostly to great interest. She is startlingly intelligent and though she looks a bit got-down physically, walking with the classic upper-class flamingo gait, she attacks life with exuberance and tough-mindedness when it comes to the crunch, and there is no masochism in her. Her focus on the things she finds absorbing is tranquil and shrewd. All the same, she is fairly far removed from ordinary attention to the practicalities of how to exist, let alone of how to do well. Her areas of abstractedness and her hatred of go-getting people make her job in a business-efficiency firm anomalous, comic, harrowing, and eventually combustible. She has a temperamental dislike of ambition.

This time the ringing on BOB's phone has been hers. ALEX holds on, lying down on her bed with a glass in her hand. Her flat has one big room with a gallery around the top half. There are books up there, and waiting in piles to be put into nearly finished shelves beside her low couch double bed. They are also along one bottom wall and piled on a desk. There are a baby grand piano, and furniture that is a mixture of valuable family pieces and Portobello Road, looking pleasant and absent-minded.

12

FRIDAY

When there is no reply to her call, her calm inexplicably explodes. She is apparently about to scatter like a rocket. She simultaneously bursts off the bed and looks àt her watch while she undoes the cap of an aspirin bottle with one hand and pulls the cotton wool out of the top with her teeth. Takes aspirins with water, gagging as she speaks to ANSWERING SERVICE.

ALEX

Oh Christ.

She is a bit pissed, but it is hard to tell. She dials again.

ALEX

Is that the answering service? Look, I'm terribly late. It's Alex Greville. My watch has stopped. What's the time?
> *(she is putting on her shoes as she talks and changing her bag)*

If Mr. Elkin rings, tell him I'm on my way and I had to booze with a client who's had the push . . .
> *(she upsets ashtray and doesn't pick it up)*

I tried to get him, Mr. Elkin, but he's gone already. Is the traffic bad?

Shot of same ANSWERING SERVICE—profile of head.

ALEX

Yuh; well, of course, it would be different round you. Worse, of course.
> *(amused)*

. . . Like your weather . . . Goodbye.

Sets her watch and throws things into a half-packed grip—books, jeans, children's books that she takes out of a bookshop paper bag.

ALEX'S KITCHEN.

Neat. Not at all scruffy. Shelves are in the middle of being built. She holds her head and makes herself some instant coffee in a hurry, waiting for the tap water to

13

be as hot as possible. The coffee is then too hot to drink and she cools it with cold tap water.

ALEX'S STUDIO STAIRS.

ALEX runs down the stairs and out of the studio.

The sound of a man singing "I Must Go Down to the Sea Again" floats out into the yard from the studio below ALEX's. Upright piano accompaniment.

ALEX'S CAR (A TRIUMPH).

Driving to Greenwich through Trafalgar Square and Fleet Street and eventually over Blackfriars Bridge. Impatience. Traffic jams. ALEX keeps looking at her watch.

> OVERHEARD CAR RADIO
> . . . The Chancellor of the Exchequer said today that as long as the present wage explosion continues, the balance of trade must be seriously affected and there will be a considerable threat to foreign exchange rates.

ALEX MEMORY SHOT OF HERSELF ALONE IN HER OFFICE AT NIGHT.

Radio sound over.

> OVERHEARD CAR RADIO
> . . . threatened steel strike. A Treasury spokesman said today that unless the disastrous wage spiral can be halted the purchasing power of the pound will be dramatically affected.

Now ALEX is on the telephone to ALVA HODSON in the HODSONS' open-plan kitchen. Both in close-up. ALEX looking troubled.

> ALVA
> You're not bothered about the kids? They like you—

FRIDAY

ALEX

—No—

ALVA

It'll be nice for both of you—trust me—

The parent HODSONS, ALVA and BILL, are an agreeable radical couple without much sense of the ridiculous. They think that ALEX and BOB should get married and have kids, and they have asked them to take over their house this weekend to promote the idea. Circular pan around the HODSON kitchen and conservatory, following TIMOTHY HODSON, who is tooting on a recorder. There are four other HODSON OFFSPRING. He skips through them and we see the room as he goes: a mixture of enlightened toys, Victorian furniture, priapic African sculpture, card indexes, and a flagon of cider. The HODSON MONKEY is eating a peanut on a pile of left-wing pamphlets.

ALEX IN A PUB EN ROUTE. CONSECUTIVE TIME, REALITY. TALKING TO LUCY HODSON, AGED NINE.

ALEX is at a coin box in the pub, leaning against the wall. The pub clock says 7:30.

ALEX

Is Bob there?

LUCY

He's a bit furious you're not here yet.

ALEX

Tell him not to be grumpy. Tell him I'm . . . tell Mummy I hope I haven't held her up and I'm hurrying.

White frames.

Clock at 7:55.

15

FRIDAY

Held shot of ALEX leaning against the pub wall for a long time. She can't really hurry. Mysteriously stalled.

Sounds of money on the bar and in the drawer of the cash till.

> FIRST MAN ON BAR STOOL
> *(disgusted)*
> "Disastrous wage spiral." They could afford to pay the railwaymen a decent wage, you'd think. See how much they spend on Prince Charles.

> SECOND MAN ON BAR STOOL
> That's promotion. That's public relations.

> FIRST MAN ON BAR STOOL
> What did we win the war for? They're doing better than we are. Bloody Boches.

> ALEX
> *(to MAN on bar stool in a different voice, submerged, struggling, slow)*
> Is that clock right, do you know?

> SECOND MAN ON BAR STOOL
> Just about.

> FIRST MAN ON BAR STOOL
> I've got a son emigrated to Canada.

> ALEX
> Surely it's miles fast, isn't it?

The MAN shrugs. The FIRST MAN is younger, with a black leather motor-bike jacket on.

THE OUTSIDE OF THE HODSONS' HOUSE. NIGHT.

Four of the kids are screaming out of different windows. ALEX drives up in her Triumph behind the HODSONS'

16

station wagon as the HODSONS, PROFESSOR JOHNS, and
BOB come out of the lighted doorway and down the
path. PROFESSOR JOHNS is a black African sociologist.
ALVA, a pretty woman of about thirty-four with an ebul-
lient style and a tired face, does sociological studies with
her husband, BILL HODSON. What follows is a back-
ground jumble of throw-away apologies and the HOD-
SONS' yelled explanations of humour. Uppermost, intimacy drawing BOB and ALEX together.

                          ALEX
I'm so sorry—

                          ALVA
It couldn't matter less, darling—

                          BILL
It's *better* to arrive there late—

                          BOB
        (affectionately)
Two bleeding hours, miss. You're never late. What
happened?

                          ALEX
I couldn't get started—

Meanwhile, BILL and ALVA are kissing her and she
shakes PROFESSOR JOHNS' hand.

                          ALEX
        (to PROFESSOR JOHNS*)*
How do you do. I really am terribly sorry.

BILL starts to put cases into the back of the station
wagon. KENYATTA, the HODSON bulldog, runs out to
the car and barges into ALEX violently.

                          ALVA
        (fondly)
Oh, he recognises you. He's glad to see you.

17

FRIDAY

ALVA climbs into the driving seat and PROFESSOR JOHNS gets in beside her.

> ALEX
> *(to BOB)*
> They won't be there till midnight.

> BOB
> *(softly)*
> Well, what's the difference?

ALVA and BILL kiss ALEX goodbye from the car.

> BILL
> The late Miss Greville.

ALVA laughs immensely at this non-joke and cranes her head through the window to shout at the CHILDREN.

> ALVA
> Papa made a joke.

> TIMOTHY
> *(shouting from window)*
> What?

> ALVA
> *(shouting louder)*
> Papa made a joke.

> LUCY
> *(bawling)*
> No, silly, Timothy meant what was the *joke?*

The concentration is now on BOB and ALEX trying to get a bit of privacy among the hubbub. ALEX crosses herself.

> ALEX
> What sort of a day did you have otherwise?

18

FRIDAY

BOB

Better than yours, maybe. There's someone interested in the bubble-tubes.

ALEX

(soft)
Clever you.

ALVA

(overlapping in a yell to LUCY)
He said to Alex "The late Miss Greville."

Hilarity from LUCY. Hilarity from the HODSONS. BOB
raises his eyebrows. The PROFESSOR smiles, looking at
the map.

BOB

(to ALEX)
You look a bit tired.

ALEX

I'm fine.

BOB

Bad day?

ALEX

(makes a face)
Busy-busy, not useful-busy.

LUCY

(shouting to the car between laughs)
Oh, well done, Papa. She is *terrifically* late.

ALVA

(bawling to LUCY)
Darling, the joke is that she isn't late meaning dead.

LUCY

(to ALVA, *shouting)*
I already saw that part.

19

KENYATTA runs again to ALEX and nearly knocks her over.

> ALVA
> *(looking at* KENYATTA, *to* ALEX*)*
> You know he's eaten already? You know he only has one meal a day?

> ALEX
> *(patiently)*
> Two pounds. Two pounds of raw tomorrow. I think I've got it.

ALVA waves goodbye and turns on the ignition.

> ALVA
> *(to* ALEX and the CHILDREN, *shouting)*
> Promise not to let the economic crisis spoil the weekend.

The car doesn't start the first time.

> ALVA
> *(to* BOB *and* ALEX*)*
> It's worrying about the cost-of-living index, isn't it? Oh, by the way, John-Stuart's milk is in the fridge.

> BILL
> *(head out of back of station wagon, waving to* ALEX *and* BOB *as car goes off)*
> Be a good family.

KIDS wave goodbye raucously long after the car is out of earshot. "Così" starts over next shot.

As the Hodson car drives off, ALVA turns to BILL.

> ALVA
> Our old mate the doctor wouldn't turn up un-asked, would he?

20

FRIDAY

Long pause after the car has gone. BOB and ALEX hold their positions and then walk to the front door. On the threshold BOB waits. ALEX has her head down, neck forward, hands in pockets. Then she touches his cheek.

> ALEX
>
> What are you thinking?

BOB makes affectionate "nothing" reply with his face.

> ALEX
>
> Sure?

HODSONS' BEDROOM. NIGHT.

Start on ALEX coming out of the bathroom door wearing dressing gown over nightdress, brushing her hair. BOB is already in bed watching the Anglican Epilogue on TV.

> CLERGYMAN
> *(on television)*
> . . . and many of you, I know, prefer sports pro-grammes to any others. So do I. We all like to cheer the winning side. But I'm not asking you to come to Christ's side because it's the winning side. Christ doesn't take sides. He doesn't judge. He cheers for you as much when you win as when you lose—

BOB turns the sound off. CLERGYMAN continues, silent.

> BOB
> *(improvising for the CLERGYMAN)*
> When I was first following Christ I was terrified he'd make me give up football. Now I know you can score a goal to the glory of God, or miss it to the glory of God.

ALEX crosses to the mirror and looks in it with her back to BOB. She brushes her hair back.

21

BOB

Don't scrape it.
(she turns and looks at him)
Come here.

She moves across room, taking off dressing gown and throwing it onto chair, and moves to the far side of the bed in a nightdress.

BOB

(heavily)
What have you got that on for? Take it off.

ALEX

(looking down at it)
Yuh, why *have* I got it on?—Maybe because of this house, subconsciously. And also because it's so bloody cold.

She takes the nightdress off. A rush of white linen across the frame.

ALEX

My god, it's freezing.

TIME-LAPSE SHOTS OF THE HODSON HOUSE AT NIGHT:

CONSERVATORY.

The MONKEY awake.

CHILDREN'S ROOM.

The baby in its cradle.

ANOTHER VIEW OF THE CHILDREN'S ROOM.

The KIDS sprawled asleep.

CORRIDOR.

KENYATTA padding about.

FRIDAY

CHILDREN'S ROOM.

LUCY lying awake.

HODSONS' BEDROOM.

BOB and ALEX under the blankets. Movement. A baby cries off-screen. Movement stops and then starts again. ALEX starts to get out of bed.

>   BOB
> If you get up, I'll kill you.

There is a knock at the door.

>   ALEX
> Yes. Who is it?

>   LUCY
> It's me. It's Lucy. Are you awake? Alex? Can you hear? Just to say I'll look after John-Stuart for you.

>   ALEX
>   *(whispering)*
> She sounds like someone's mother-in-law. Loitering.

>   LUCY
>   *(knocks again)*
> Can you hear? I can't hear if you can hear. Alex?

BOB gets out of bed naked, and moves quickly towards the door.

>   BOB
> Come in.

>   ALEX
>   *(shouts)*
> No! Stay out! Go away!

23

FRIDAY

It's all right. I'll manage.

HODSONS' KITCHEN. NIGHT.

ALEX is wearing a mohair rug from the HODSONS' bed and BOB is in pants and two long thick sweaters. The two of them are eating out of the fridge, which is packed with family food not looking very eatable. There are large posters about famine-relief on the wall.

ALEX
(with mild interest)
Do you think Alva and Bill had that disgusting eel and pumpernickel they gave us? I wonder if they'll be sick in the middle of the sociologists.

BOB
I want some milk.

ALEX
Milk? I want some wine. You get more and more like an American.

BOB
What's this?

He picks up a screw top jar with something milky in it.

ALEX
It looks special. I'll ask Lucy tomorrow.

They sit at the table and eat cheese and bread and tomatoes. A dog bays.

ALEX
How typical of them to have those posters. In *here*. To take your appetite away.

BOB
But, well, Alva does that sort of thing.

24

FRIDAY

ALEX

Why the hell did we come?

BOB

Because you're soft.

ALEX

No, because it's a chance of a whole weekened together.
(eyeing him)
She thinks we ought to get married.

BOB

She's a sort of C.I.A. agent for happy families.
(eats)
She thinks we're her guinea pigs.

ALEX turns away and opens some wine, then looks back at BOB and holds his hand.

ALEX

Well, we're not, are we?

LUCY comes in with a heavy sigh, the BULLDOG beside her.

LUCY

You locked Kenyatta out of your bedroom. He sleeps on the bed.

ALEX

Oh. Well, I *am* sorry.

LUCY

(graciously)
I don't suppose you meant to.

ALEX

Is this milk all right for Bob to drink?

25

LUCY

It's Mummy's.

ALEX

Can't she spare it?

LUCY

It's *Mummy's,* I said, for *John-Stuart.* He isn't *weaned.*

BOB

Oh my god.

LUCY goes upstairs with the BULLDOG.

HODSONS' BEDROOM. NIGHT. GETTING LIGHTER.

The DOG is asleep on all but the top third of ALEX's side of the bed. ALEX is lying awake. BOB is dead asleep with his head under a pillow. JOHN-STUART cries and ALEX reacts. She slides her bent knees carefully out of the bed, puts on the dressing gown, and goes into the nursery.

LUCY has forestalled her. The CHILD turns the BABY over and copes with rebuking efficiency. ALEX remains on the hover at the door, silent, displaced.

DANIEL'S CONSULTING ROOM. NIGHT. GETTING LIGHTER.

(Same time as ALEX's.)
We see DANIEL's back bending down to put "Così fan Tutte" on to his complicated Hi-Fi. Close-ups of switches on the mechanism as he puts on the records and starts the music.

DANIEL looks out of his window at the garden, eating from a tube of polo mints.

BOB's geodesic sculpture looms in the garden, looking strange and rather beautiful.

FRIDAY

THE OUTSIDE OF DANIEL'S HOUSE. NIGHT.

DANIEL emptying dustbins.

HODSONS' BEDROOM. NIGHT. NEARER DAWN.

"Così" music carries over.

The DOG is still asleep in most of ALEX's place in the bed. ALEX is sitting on the windowsill watching BOB asleep. After a while she kneels on the floor beside him and kisses his hand.

SATURDAY

HODSONS' BEDROOM. MORNING.

"SATURDAY" title on frame.

CHILDREN all over the bed, singing a round, bouncing, reading the "Guardian." TIMOTHY has taken a gulp of ALEX's coffee and he is making a face at it. The BABY is asleep between the DOG's paws.

> TIMOTHY
> Eech.

> ALEX
> Serves you right for pinching my breakfast.

Pause. The KIDS look spinsterish.

> TIMOTHY
> Not *your* breakfast. Papa paid for it.

> BOB
> There's socialism for you.

> TIMOTHY
> What does he mean?

CHILDREN crawl over ALEX, smoking. Some of them have chocolate cigarettes, some pot. Indistinguishable.

SATURDAY

ALEX
(eyes closed, using a dowager's voice)
It was very nice of you to bring the tray up.

TIMOTHY
Why has she gone old?

BOB
She does it sometimes for fun in the mornings.

LUCY
(to ALEX*)*
Mummy said you'd like a lie-in together in peace.

BOB
Did she mention you lot coming in with the tray? And staying?

LUCY
We always come in here first thing.
(pause)
Then we watch Mummy and Papa have a bath together.

ALEX screams.

BOB
(to LUCY*)*
Be a good chap and piss off, will you?

LUCY
(laughs heartily)
I'm not a chap, I'm a girl.

ALEX closes her eyes in some anguish, opening them again with another thing to face entirely.

ALEX
There's the most peculiar smell in here. It's just like pot. Are you children smoking pot?

30

SATURDAY

LUCY is silent. Pause.

> LUCY
>
> *(to* ALEX*)*
> Are you a bourgeoise?

> ALEX
>
> I don't mind, but does Mummy know?
> *(pause)*

> LUCY
>
> Yes. *Well.* They keep it at the back of the records.

> TIMOTHY
>
> Behind "Tristan and Isolde."

> ALEX
>
> Yes, but does she mind?
> *(to* BOB *for advice)*
> Bob?

> BOB
>
> *(to* ALEX*)*
> I don't suppose it matters.

> ALEX
>
> *(to* BOB*)*
> No, O.K.
> *(to* LUCY*)*
> Now, about whether I'm a bourgeoise.

> BOB
>
> *(to* LUCY*)*
> She has a bourgeois father who's very grand and
> owns a lot of banks. O.K., little comrade?

> FIVE-YEAR-OLD BOY
>
> *(to* ALEX*)*
> Do you work for a living?

31

ALEX

Yes.

LUCY

What as?

BOB
(leaning back on pillows, in a jolly, swift-speaking mood, meaning to make ALEX *and himself sound as stupid to the* KIDS *as possible)*
She's a business-efficiency expert and I design plastic rubbish. So there you are, mate.

Most of the CHILDREN kill themselves with laughter. ALEX lights a Kent.

LUCY
(to TIMOTHY, *who is still giggling)*
Timothy, stop laughing, he *meant* it.

ALEX
Go away and freak out or something, can't you? And give me your nice liberal newspaper, Lucy. Is this the only one they get?

LUCY
Mummy and Papa read *all* the papers. This is the one they like in bed.

HODSONS' GARDEN, SEEN THROUGH THE WINDOW BY BOB, AND FROM THE LAWN.

BOB is looking through a prism. JOHN-STUART is in his cot. We see the BABY then through the prism: multiple JOHN-STUARTS.

CHILDREN's voices over.

ALEX is playing on the lawn with the OLDER CHILDREN and KENYATTA. After a while she looks up at the window. Something on her mind.

32

SATURDAY

HODSONS' OPEN-PLAN GROUND FLOOR.

BOB is sitting at a loom, fiddling with some gadget of his own. Preoccupation. ALEX is in the foreground, sitting on the sofa with her legs up, looking at him and thinking. Pause. He looks at his watch.

ALEX

Is it too early for a Bloody Mary?

BOB

You sound very cheery.

ALEX

I came to a decision about ten seconds ago.

BOB

What?

ALEX

(sounding fine)
I'm going to give myself the sack at the office.

BOB

What?

ALEX

Quit. Pack it in. I'm fed up with grooming people to be thrusters.

BOB fiddles with the shuttle of the loom.

ALEX

What's eating you?
(pause. Change of voice. Soft)
Hey.

BOB

Are you doing it because of me?

33

SATURDAY

He moves to the mantelpiece. The shot moves round, and ALEX's head follows BOB. Through the following lines we see only the back of her head, in quarter-profile. We can see BOB's briefcase at the end of the sofa.

ALEX

No, my duck. You turn everything to yourself.

BOB silently rummages in his briefcase. He doesn't particularly like getting near her at this huffy point but he needs the thing. Pause.

ALEX

You're not very chatty, flower.

BOB

I've got to go out for a bit.

Pause.

ALEX

Is that so difficult to say to me?

BOB

I've got to go into town.

ALEX

Look, you want to piss off, right? Only don't tell me you've got to work.

He goes towards the door.

ALEX

Wait—wait—wait. Let me guess. What day of the week is it? Saturday. Saturday. I think you're going to see a certain person whose name begins with— D. Whose name begins with D—*A*.
(cheerful voice)
Am I getting warm?

BOB is looking at his watch and counting her out.

34

SATURDAY

Time's up.

Well, fine. You can give me a ring. No, you won't
have time. Anyway, take the car.

He gets near the door and she throws the car keys at
him. BOB throws them back and grins at her, in hope of
a grin in return.

(denying him that)
Have fun with.

Close-up at last on her face when the door has banged
behind him. Stricken.

DANIEL'S CONSULTING ROOM. CONSECUTIVE
TIME.

He is sitting behind his desk. MIDDLE-AGED WOMAN
PATIENT.

It's the dirt he brings home I can't stand.

(picking the words carefully for her)
How long is it since you led a normal married life
with him?

The PATIENT looks around his room.

This place is kept nice.

DANIEL waits and then pushes her.

How long is it, though?

SATURDAY

PATIENT

I can't complain.

DANIEL

You mean he hasn't been near you for a long time.
(pause)
Or is it that you haven't wanted him to?

PATIENT

He never interfered with me without call.

DANIEL

(after pause)
Have you ever thought of leaving him?

PATIENT

*(in a panic, resisting such a dead-right sugges-
tion)*
It'd kill him.
(pause)
We don't divorce, our family.

DANIEL

But has it crossed your mind? Sometimes people
survive better apart. Even after a long time together.

PATIENT

(defensive)
What do you know about it? You're not married,
are you?

DANIEL

No.

PATIENT

Well then.
(pause, sad)
Too late to start again, and that's the pity of it. I
like your little elephants.
(pause)
Do *you* think I should leave him?

36

SATURDAY

DANIEL

It needn't be for good. It needn't be anything
definite. Couldn't you go and stay with friends?

PATIENT

I haven't got any . . . not that sort . . . We never
had time for neighbours. It'd kill him, I tell you.
Who'd look after him?

DANIEL picks up one of his elephants.

PATIENT

It was never that sort of thing between us . . .
Not what you're saying . . . nothing physical. He
just said to me when he proposed, do you think
we'd make a go of it? And I said, when he'd got
a decent place to offer me, and there it is.
   (pause)
We've always been good to one another.

He writes a prescription, and puts the elephant into the
prescription envelope.

PEMBROKE SQUARE.

BOB walks towards DANIEL's house, carrying his briefcase.

DANIEL'S HOUSE—THE CONSULTING ROOM,
PASSAGE AND FRONT DOOR.

PATIENT

Did I speak out of turn?

DANIEL

Oh, no. Let me know about the headaches.

PATIENT

Thanks very much.
   (puts envelope in her handbag)
Good of you to see me on a Saturday. A doctor

37

never rests, though, does he? It must be interesting,
seeing people.
(they go out into the hall)

DANIEL

I could do with a holiday.

PATIENT
(she doesn't listen to him)
It's a calling, isn't it?

Unseen by her, BOB opens the front door, using his own
key. The corridor gets momentarily brighter with the
door opening. He goes into the kitchen, raising eyebrows
infinitesimally as DANIEL shows the WOMAN PATIENT
out, who is crying.

DANIEL
(shaking her hand at the front door)
Next week. Hold on.

DANIEL'S KITCHEN.

BOB waiting. DANIEL comes in.

DANIEL
(changed voice)
Jesus, I wish they wouldn't all cry.

DANIEL and BOB kiss each other.

DANIEL
I didn't expect to see you this weekend.

BOB
You're working and it's Saturday.

DANIEL
She said it was a calling. It always makes me want
to be a house painter.

38

SATURDAY

BOB

Are you all right?

They look at each other. DANIEL starts to move into the passage towards the consulting room, BOB following him.

DANIEL

Christ, I'm flaked. I've had three nervous crack-ups, two cases of the pox, two German measles, and a case of advanced leukaemia, and all on a *Saturday*.

DANIEL'S CONSULTING ROOM.

DANIEL sits at his desk, lying down a bit in the chair, watching BOB move around the room. BOB straightens a picture and moves some ornaments and opens and closes the door on the little fridge, which has drugs in it. Then he looks at one of the paintings on the wall opposite DANIEL.

BOB

So you finally bought it. Possessions, possessions.

DANIEL

They told me it would be an investment.

BOB

It's nice.

BOB walks out into the garden to look at his sculpture.

He presses a switch inside the French doors before he goes out and the sculpture lights up.

DANIEL stands by the billowing curtains, watching.

BOB

How's it bearing up?

DANIEL

Fine. I had it on last night in the rain.

BOB

I think it's the best thing I've ever done. Do you think the Americans will like it?

DANIEL

Yes, I should think they'd eat it. In fact, are you sure they haven't thought of it already?

BOB
(tinkering with the sculpture)
Somebody seems interested. Can you switch it off? Now on! Off!—They keep telephoning from New York. . . . Now on . . .
(the sculpture lights up again)
. . . if we could do something like this on a fantastic scale—

DANIEL

Would it mean you going there?

BOB

Yuh, but if I went, it wouldn't be for long.

DANIEL's outside phone rings. He makes a face. So does BOB. DANIEL picks up the phone and listens.

DANIEL

Yes.
(then to ANSWERING SERVICE*)*
No, I'm on the line, Answering.
(pause. Listens to a patient)
He's been taking the pills, has he?

CHILD PATIENT'S MOTHER

Well, he didn't seem to like them, he can hardly swallow, I told you.

DANIEL

But didn't you—

40

SATURDAY

CHILD PATIENT'S MOTHER
(cuts in)
He's running a terrible fever.

DANIEL
That's exactly why I gave you the pills ... To bring down the *fever*. They'll *do* that—that's what they're *for* ... Yes, I think I know.

CHILD PATIENT'S MOTHER
He's running a terrible fever.

DANIEL
But Mrs. Hackett, haven't you—actually—given— *the pills I prescribed?* Why don't you just try that?

CHILD PATIENT'S MOTHER
It seemed as if it won't do him any good.

DANIEL
And let me know tomorrow morning, *but only if his fever hasn't gone down. Otherwise ring me on Monday,* right?

DANIEL puts down phone and stalks around.

BOB
How do you put up with it?

After a bit DANIEL cools down and sits.

DANIEL
Do you want a drink?
(pause)
Ice.
(pause)
How long have you got?

BOB
A while.

41

DANIEL

Is Alex hating it up there? Is Lucy putting her through it? Why on earth did you go?

BOB

Because she wanted me to.
(pause)

BOB gets off the desk.

BOB

Because I wanted to.

DANIEL

How the hell did you get away?

BOB

Because I wanted to see you.

DANIEL

Do you want a drink?

BOB has opened a book of Italian photographs.

BOB

Scotch.

HODSONS' KITCHEN. SAME TIME.

ALEX is crying. Radio on to cheer herself up. She's also been making fudge. She eats bits of it before it is cool and reads P. G. Wodehouse with her legs up on the kitchen table. Burning her fingers. The HODSONS' younger daughter, TESS, is doing a large-scale jig-saw on the floor. ALEX looks at her struggling with the pieces. She picks up TESS and takes her back to the table to sit on her lap, putting the jig-saw on the table with her other hand. TESS looks round at her remotely, and struggles off her knees to take the jig-saw back to the floor.

LUCY comes in.

42

SATURDAY

LUCY

I've come to get the fudge.

LUCY looks at the tray, nasty little inspector.

LUCY

You've *eaten* it.

ALEX

Well, it was me that wanted it in the first place, me that made it, and there's a ton of it left.

LUCY

Where's Bob?

ALEX

Out.

ALEX has another piece, burning her mouth again but pretending not to.

LUCY

When's he coming back?

ALEX

Soon. What are you all doing?

LUCY

Why don't you know *exactly* when he's coming back?

ALEX

Oh, do stop, lovey. I do know. I just can't be bothered to tell you.

LUCY

Has Bob walked out on you? I expect that's why you're overeating.

43

DANIEL'S CONSULTING ROOM.

BOB is engrossed in the book of Italian photographs. Pages of Southern Italian and Sicilian religious parades in hoods that look like the Ku Klux Klan. DANIEL comes in and looks over his shoulder.

Details of book and hands turning pages forwards and then backwards to look again at a particular photograph —Italianate devotions, a skull dressed up like a bride, political photographs.

> BOB (voice over)
> Bludgeoned into feeling something. I can't see being a fanatic, can you?

> DANIEL
> Not sure.

More pictures. Mussolini era. A child carrying a cross in a charade of Calvary.

> BOB
> Do you honestly feel Jewish?

> DANIEL
> Not much, I'm afraid.
> *(pause)*
> Except when I was at school. There were eight of us out of two hundred and fifty.
> *(pause)*
> I like chopped liver.

More pictures. Landscape, wine, fun.

> BOB
> When are we going to Italy?

Pictures of people together having a good time.

> DANIEL
> End of the month?

SATURDAY

BOB
Yuh. Could we take the car?

DANIEL
I don't see why not.

DANIEL'S BEDROOM. LATE AFTERNOON.

DANIEL in bed. Two-shot with BOB coming out of the bathroom door, dressed.

Close-up on BOB coming towards DANIEL, taking off his sweater.

Cut to close-up of them in bed. Naked shoulders.

A telephone rings.

Close-up of DANIEL's face.

Cut to his hand switching off the control button of the ringing.

The sound continues faintly from the downstairs telephones.

Close-up of BOB's and DANIEL's faces waiting for the ANSWERING SERVICE to pick up.

Everything stops for answering services.

DANIEL
Three. Four. I told them to pick it up at three. Six. Seven. Ye gods, eight. They're never going to answer it.

Eventually the ringing stops.

TUBE TRAIN. EVENING.

BOB is standing propped in a tube reading the "Evening Standard." We see him through a gang of cheery people coming back from football at Tottenham.

45

Then he gets out through the crowd and makes for his connection back to Greenwich. He stops at a gadgety type-machine and punches out his name two ways in tin. "Bob Elkin." "Elkin."

HODSONS' DRAWING ROOM. NIGHT.

ALEX is sight-reading "The Jolly Farmer" from the kids' piano music. There is a plate of fudge on the side of the piano. After playing for a time she suddenly looks round, aware of someone's eyes on her, and sees the MONKEY sitting in an armchair staring at her, apparently infuriated by the music. She throws a piece of fudge at the animal to send him back into the conservatory. At this point the lights suddenly fuse. She gropes her way towards the door and swears.

HODSONS' PASSAGE.

BOB is back and at the fuse box, up on a ladder. ALEX leans against the opposite wall of the passage, pointing a torch at him in a caustic mood. One light only is still working, outside the back door at the far end of the passage.

> ALEX
> Do put the main switch off. You'll electrocute yourself.

She holds the torch up for him.

> BOB
> Do you think I don't know how to mend a fuse?

> ALEX
> *(factual, affectionate)*
> Yes.

He pulls the main switch off and the light at the far end of the passage is now, of course, dead. ALEX passes him

46

the torch. BOB looks at a fuse and picks it apart. He puts it back, pulls the main switch on, and the light in the passage is still dead. She goes on leaning against the ladder to stop it slipping.

BOB

Why the hell don't we have those American fuses in England?

ALEX

Darling, as soon as you get yourself into a jam you say it's better in America. How do you *know?* You've never been there.

BOB is fiddling with the passage fuse and has managed to make it function again.

ALEX

Well done.

BOB

(irritated)
I'm useless at this.

ALEX

(on edge about the day)
Couldn't matter less.

BOB

Don't push it. Please don't push it.

ALEX

I never mentioned him.

BOB

Use his *name* if you can't resist bringing him up.

ALEX

I didn't bring him up.

47

> BOB
>
> No, but I could hear you thinking it.
> *(pause)*
> Piss off to the kids' floor and see if anything works
> up there, will you?

ALEX stomps away, keeping the torch.

> BOB
>
> *(shouts after her)*
> Leave me the torch.

> ALEX
>
> *(shouts)*
> You can see by the candles.

HODSONS' HALL AND STAIRS. TORCHLIGHT.

Camera follows ALEX upstairs. She is in a flaming spat
and bangs her head against the heel of her hand when
she gets to the top of the stairs, stamping her feet and
swearing. She recovers a bit and starts switching on
each one of the row of lights on the landing panel.

HODSONS' BASEMENT. CANDLELIGHT.

Reaction shot of BOB hearing her yelling upstairs.

> BOB
>
> *(shouting at her)*
> Does that work?

> ALEX
>
> *(shouting out of shot)*
> NO!

HODSONS' HALL AND STAIRS. TORCHLIGHT TO FULL ELECTRIC LIGHT.

> BOB
>
> *(shouts out of shot)*
> What about that one?

SATURDAY

ALEX

(shouts)
YES!

The lights have suddenly blazed and she is caught as if she were in a photographic flare. The KIDS wake up and yell and the BULLDOG barks. LUCY appears, blinking.

LUCY
Is Bob back? Is everything all right?

ALEX

(going downstairs)
Shouldn't you be asleep?

HODSONS' BASEMENT PASSAGE. CANDLE-LIGHT.

ALEX comes back into the basement. A dusty naked bulb suddenly goes on by BOB's hand as he fiddles with the fuse box.

BOB

(breezy)
Eureka. That one can't have gone on since the Crimean War.

ALEX
I missed you.

BOB

(what, after all that racket from her?)
Upstairs?

ALEX
Today.

BOB

(coming down first three steps)
Don't go on at me like some possessive *wife*.
(comes down the rest of the steps)

49

SATURDAY

ALEX

Well, I *feel* a bit like a possessive wife, after being left alone with five children, one monkey, one dog—

BOB

(overlapping)
—you've never complained about it before.

ALEX

Well, I've never been left around before in the middle of what was supposed to be a proper week-end—

BOB

—you should have said something about it in the first place.
(pause)
I know you don't think you're getting enough of me, but you're getting all there is.

ALEX

Perhaps you shouldn't spread yourself so thin.

BOB

(walking away)
Oh, drop it.

BATHROOM OFF HODSONS' BEDROOM. NIGHT.

ALEX is crouched on the floor with her elbows on her knees and her chin in her hands. She looks round and watches BOB in the shower through the shower panel. He comes out. She puts her arms out to him and hugs him.

ALEX

Sorry, sorry, sorry, sorry, sorry.

BOB

Silly tart.

Image of his wet back with her hands on it.

SATURDAY

DANIEL DRIVING. NIGHT.

Alternating shots of old London buildings and of neon
financial headlines, seen through wind-screen wipers.
He draws up at a traffic light. A GLASWEGIAN MAN is
standing on a traffic island. He grins into the car.
DANIEL looks across at him. The MAN comes over.
DANIEL startlingly locks the car doors and waits for the
green light. The MAN comes over to him and his face
looms into the driving-seat side-window. A COP watches
from the other side of the road.

                    SCOTSMAN
     I said hello.

DANIEL turns his head to the steering wheel.

                    SCOTSMAN
          (louder)
     You don't remember me.

DANIEL looks round and speaks loudly through the
window.

                    DANIEL
     No, I don't.

                    SCOTSMAN
          (shouting)
     Look, don't pretend you don't remember me.

The SCOTSMAN bashes the car window with his closed
fist.

                    DANIEL
     Stop it!

The SCOTSMAN bashes the car window harder with his
fist, and then stops and nurses his knuckles. The POLICE-
MAN comes over to the car.

51

SATURDAY

> SCOTSMAN

Ah, Christ.

> DANIEL
> *(unlocks car door)*

Well, get in.

> SCOTSMAN
> *(gets in)*

He'll nab me.

DANIEL quickly examines the hand as the COP comes up. DANIEL winds down his window.

> DANIEL

It's all right, officer. I'm a doctor. He's hurt his hand. He thought he knew me. I'll get it bandaged. He didn't see the window was up.

The COP nods reluctantly, sceptical. But DANIEL sounds like a man in command.

DANIEL drives off. He doesn't glance at the MAN.

> SCOTSMAN

How've you been keeping?

DANIEL is silent.

> SCOTSMAN

My hand hurts. Might be broken.

> DANIEL

You're moving the fingers. Bruise, that's all.

> SCOTSMAN
> *(leaning back in car, spreading himself)*

Just stop pretending you don't remember.
> *(pause)*

SATURDAY

DANIEL

I remember very well indeed.
(he drives coolly and fast)
Actually, you were pissed the *last* time.

SCOTSMAN

Are we going back to your place, then?

The car passes a shop with one of BOB's sculpture gadgets in it.

DANIEL

No, we are *not* going back to my place. I'm dropping you off. And on the way I'm going to the chemist to get some pain-killers for you.

DANIEL starts, unwisely, to overtake a car. Headlights flashing in opposite direction.

SCOTSMAN

Oh, well. For Christ's sake look where you're going. You're not much of a driver. *Doctor.*
(pause)
What are you thinking?

DANIEL

(hard voice)
I was thinking about my *brother*. And he's *dead*.
(pause)

SCOTSMAN

Are you in love?

DANIEL

Probably.

He goes past an all-night chemist and parks down a side road.

SATURDAY

SCOTSMAN
(mocking)
Poor old Danny.

DANIEL
Christ, you even remember my name.

The SCOTSMAN winks.

ALL-NIGHT CHEMIST. NIGHT.

Bleached-out and over-exposed. Scene in shades of white. The usual Saturday night small-hours sight: Indians, Pakistanis, junkies, queens. Everything seems a little at a distance, slow and opiate. Emphasis on white overalls and people too tired, isolated, or in need of a fix to speak. Frigid pale faces and lips that look cyanose, like clowns'. DANIEL stands in the queue at the prescription counter. He writes out a prescription on a piece of paper from his wallet while he is waiting. A thin JUNKIE of about seventeen with a prescription for heroin is collapsed with his head on his chest. DANIEL is tough enough, but at this time of night, on this night in particular, he is less inured than usual. A YOUNG WOMAN speaks softly and urgently to another ASSISTANT.

WOMAN CUSTOMER
. . . Cough pastilles that are safe for a child but very strong. She won't stop coughing. She isn't three, quite. She keeps being sick.

DANIEL meanwhile looks constantly at the BOY getting high in the corner.

PHARMACIST
(to DANIEL, *thinking that* DANIEL *is trying to pick the* BOY *up)*
Yes?

DANIEL hands over the prescription and still eyes the BOY. What he feels is concern, but the PHARMACIST misreads it. It is that sort of night.

PHARMACIST
(contemptuously)
This isn't signed. Could be a forgery. Just an initial.

DANIEL
(points)
That's the way I sign my name. I'm a doctor. Doctors have writing like this.

PHARMACIST
You a doctor?

(It *is* that sort of night, certainly.)

DANIEL
I know it's hard to read. H—I—R—S—H.

PHARMACIST
Where did you get this prescription paper?

DANIEL
Look, it's the same signature as my driving licence, isn't it?

The PHARMACIST looks at the driving licence and hands it back sourly. It is unsigned.

DANIEL
Oh. I must have forgotten to sign it. All right, I'll get my instrument case from the car to identify myself. If you're going to be difficult.

PARKING PLACE BY THE CHEMIST.

DANIEL opens his car. The GLASWEGIAN has disappeared from it, with DANIEL's case.

A copy of "The Lancet" is on the driving seat. The words "BETTER LUCK NEXT TIME" are written across the cover in big capital letters.

SUNDAY

LONDON. NIGHT STREETS.

DANIEL driving his car.

Cut to back-reference shot of multiplying headlights flashing into DANIEL's eyes. The title "SUNDAY" comes up on the screen.

Go to black.

Black screen clears as if hands were coming away from the face.

DANIEL is in his bed, hands coming away from his eyes, waking up.

Cut to his hand on window blind, letting light into the shot.

DANIEL comes downstairs, pulling up blinds at various windows and turning off a couple of lights left burning.

THE OUTSIDE OF DANIEL'S HOUSE. SUNDAY MORNING.

Closer shot of DANIEL inside the house front door, un-doing the chain and fiddling with the double lock. The camera pulls back as he comes out in his dressing gown to pick up the milk and his newspapers. A MAN in white shorts runs by, arms pumping; one of England's frail-

57

looking nuts, tough as nails. DANIEL puts the milk inside the front door and opens the newspapers. He has two copies of the "News of the World."

The door of the next-door house has just opened and CAPTAIN SHACKLETON comes out, also in a dressing gown, with a scarf tucked into the neck. Dapper. He picks up his own newspapers, and DANIEL and he greet each other simultaneously.

<table>
<tr><td>DANIEL
(raising voice)
Morning.</td><td>CAPTAIN SHACKLETON
(raising voice)
Morning.</td></tr>
</table>

> DANIEL
>
> I've got two "News of the Worlds." Is one of them yours?

> CAPTAIN SHACKLETON
> (looking at his bundle)
> I've got two "Observers."

They exchange newspapers with polite smiles. DANIEL looks congratulatorily at CAPTAIN SHACKLETON's window boxes.

> DANIEL
>
> Your bulbs are very far on, aren't they?

CAPTAIN SHACKLETON turns away with the "Observer" on the top of his pile, reading it. We see the muted political headline about the financial crisis. DANIEL turns away with the "News of the World" on the top of his pile. We see a headline about a defrocked vicar.

GREENWICH STREET WITH A VIEW TOWARDS CHURCH IN DISTANCE.

BOB and ALEX with newspapers under their arms are going for a walk with the CHILDREN and the BULLDOG.

SUNDAY

LUCY is pushing the pram. There are other PEOPLE in the street—other FAMILIES—with MOTHERS and FATHERS pushing prams. We see, hidden from BOB and ALEX, a small gang of well-dressed CHILDREN with pieces of a broken milk bottle, going along a row of parked cars and scraping the paint with their home-made weapons. A couple of thousand quids'-worth of damage, maybe.

BOB and ALEX pass a WOMAN bending over a pram with a BABY in it, making goo-goo noises at it.

> WOMAN
> How old is he?

> MOTHER
> Three weeks. She's a girl.

> WOMAN
> You can tell, can't you.

GREENWICH OBSERVATORY.

BOB and ALEX are at the telescope. BOB is hogging it. Enlargements of the CHILDREN. TIMOTHY is throwing sticks for KENYATTA. LUCY contemptuously takes over from him and throws the stick far better, as well she may. She wags a finger at KENYATTA and makes him sit on command. Hard discipline. ALEX makes a face. BOB laughs at her.

> ALEX
> *(thankful sigh)*
> Distance.

A GREENWICH HILL. DAY.

LUCY is wheeling the pram again. ALEX and BOB are swinging one of the younger children off the ground on a count of one, two, three. After a couple of times they release the CHILD, who runs around with the others. BOB takes ALEX's hand and LUCY glances at that. The little matchmaker is suddenly jealous, shut out. She abandons the pram and plays hopping games on the pavement. ALEX takes over the pram.

LUCY

Look at me.

BOB

Yuh.

LUCY
(to BULLDOG)
Come on, Kenyatta.

ALEX

See if you can beat him up to the next lamp-post.

LUCY and BULLDOG run excitedly, not to the lamp-post but across the street diagonally.

A lorry turns the corner, jolting uphill.

ALEX

Lucy! Run quick!

The lorry misses LUCY but hits the DOG. No screech of brakes. Softly over. Moment of impact played on ALEX's face. She has her hand to her mouth.

Close-up on LUCY's face. A real child suddenly.

LORRY DRIVER
(yelling, climbing out of lorry, frightened)
What the hell do you think you're doing? Letting children—

BOB

Belt up.

60

LORRY DRIVER

—arse about all over the road. Lucky for you we weren't all killed.

BOB

Look, belt up and help, will you? Empty that sack.

The LORRY DRIVER does as he's told.

Close-up on ALEX and BOB bending down over the DOG, with ALEX's hair swinging over BOB's cheek. He holds the hair against his face for a second.

ALEX
(low voice to him)
I'll get them home.

She moves the CHILDREN away and walks them home. She looks back and then sees LUCY looking back too. ALEX picks her up and hugs her.

BOB
(shouting to them)
Start a game, and Lucy play my turn until I get there.

Closer shot of the disappearing party. BOB is now in the far distance with the body of the DOG visible beside his feet. He makes the LORRY DRIVER wait with him until the CHILDREN have turned the corner. Then he wraps up the DOG's body in a sack.

HODSONS' KITCHEN.

BOB and the CHILDREN are playing a game of picture consequences at the table. Folding of paper as the CHILDREN draw various heads, bodies, and legs, and then pleasure when they undo the concertinas and inspect the whole figures. LUCY is shaky and tear-stained. BOB is doing well with the kids. There is a chill in the

61

air in spite of the game, and a closing of ranks. ALEX comes in.

> ALEX
>
> I've just rung Mummy about Kenyatta. Would it be nice to speak to her?

> LUCY
>
> No, we're all right.

But one of the smaller children looks relieved, gets off BOB's knee, and runs to the phone.

Shot of LUCY at the HODSONS' table, drawing something we can't see. Tear-stained. BOB leaning over her.

HODSONS' BATHROOM. SUNDAY, LATE AFTERNOON.

ALEX is looking for a pill.

> BOB (voice over)
>
> Alex?

> ALEX
>
> I thought I'd try going to sleep. I can't find a pill.

BOB is reflected in the bathroom mirror. He comes towards her and takes her in his arms.

> ALEX
>
> I keep thinking it could have been Lucy.

> BOB
>
> Well, it wasn't.

He strokes her forehead.

> BOB
>
> Slow down.

SUNDAY

HODSONS' BEDROOM.

Now ALEX is in bed, throwing one leg out of the sheets. BOB is sitting on the floor next to the bed against a couple of pillows. He is looking at her and drawing sometimes on a clip-board. Pre-cue sound of air-raid siren. We go into a sequence of Consequence drawings muddled up with gas-mask memories. Material of bad dreams.

Filter shot of LUCY running in ALEX's imagination in the Greenwich street—running towards the distant figure of the DOG, without BOB there now.

Memory shot of ALEX at LUCY's age, running down the hundred-yard corridor of her parents' block of flats. The corridor is lined with black-out curtains. She chases out and then down Portland Place, seen from the same angle as the Greenwich street. She is in schoolgirl uniform and carrying her father's gas mask. Her FATHER, in back view, is bicycling away down Portland Place: a touching and dignified figure wearing bicycle clips, with a briefcase banging against the handlebars. The London street is full of bicycles. Hardly any traffic. (Petrol rationing.)

Filter shot of heads in gas masks during an imagined gas raid, ALEX's FATHER on his bicycle, without a mask, coughing.

Shot of one of the HODSON CHILDREN's completed Consequence figures. There is a man's head at the top, a drawing by LUCY of Kenyatta's body and tail, and a drawing by ANOTHER CHILD of Kenyatta's legs curled up under him. Grotesque image, like the heads in gas masks.

> BOB (voice over)
> Can anybody tell me how to draw a boot? I don't seem to be any good at feet.

Filter shot of ALEX in schoolgirl uniform, earlier in her recollection, seen in the dining room of what later turns

63

out to be still her parents' home. Breakfast with her
FATHER, sitting close together at one end of the table
seen later. The air-raid siren goes. MR. GREVILLE gets
up and says, "Look after yourself, Alex. I'll do the
Latin tonight." Kisses her goodbye. She watches him
out of the window, unpadlocking his bicycle from the
railings outside. She sees that he has forgotten his gas
mask, which is hanging on the back of his chair, and
starts running after him. BOB's voice, in reality, follows
the recollection of MR. GREVILLE's voice.

> BOB (voice over)
> Lucy, that's a very good middle of a horse.

Shot of another grotesque Consequence assembly with
KENYATTA's head fixed to the body of a horse and then
to a man's trousered legs with big army boots.

Filter shot of ALEX as child running after the now nearly
vanished figure of MR. GREVILLE.

> ALEX
> *(as child)*
> Daddy, your gas mask!

He doesn't hear. She grabs a bicycle, but it is padlocked
to the railings. She runs after him, panting. Bumping
into people. She seizes someone.

> ALEX
> My father's forgotten his gas mask. He'll be gassed.
> *(crying)*
> He'll get killed.

The PASSER-BY shrugs and replies in Polish.

HODSONS' BEDROOM. SUNDAY AFTERNOON.

BOB gets up to cover ALEX with the bedclothes. There
are close-ups of her beautiful face, intercut with close-

ups of BOB's pencil making circling shapes, round and
round, like the movement of the harmonograph that we
saw in his flat earlier on. The last shot of his doodling
melts into the sphere of a telephone dial. BOB telephoning: BOB the not dream-ridden. His memory is shorter
than hers and he can always find exits.

> BOB
> *(whispering so as not to wake ALEX)*
> Tommy there?
> *(pause)*
> Hi. Has that thing come back from the workshop
> yet? I still can't think how to hang it. It needs so
> much bleeding room. Look, bring it up, will you?
> Where I told you, yuh.

Go to black. Pause.

Black screen slowly merges into semi-discernible shapes
of HODSON bedroom. Much time has passed. ALEX has
been right out for a long time. There are faint voices
from downstairs and upstairs. The door is ajar. There
is a glow from the windows of the houses opposite. She
is quite lost for a bit. Where am I, what day?

HODSONS' KITCHEN. EVENING.

ALEX is coming down the stairs. She takes in a scene
that looks like the HODSON household just as she has
always known it. ALEX usurped. Wide-shot panorama
of chaos with ALVA in imperturbable command of it.
Cases and typewriter-lid unpacked from the car are on
the floor. ALVA is cooking at high speed for unidentified
numbers. The MONKEY sits on the work-tops. The CHIL-
DREN are at one end of the table finishing their supper,
supervised by LUCY. PROFESSOR JOHNS types at the
other end of the table. TIMOTHY has left his place and is
banging a tambourine and an African bongo drum around
PROFESSOR JOHNS. ALVA is shouting at the CHILDREN to
get them to bed.

SUNDAY

ALVA
Bed—bed—bed! Timothy, stop it! Come on, bed!

CHILDREN
Not yet, Mummy! No! Not sleepy!

ALEX has entered.

ALEX
I'm so sorry. I must have been flat out for hours.

ALVA
We crept up but you looked as if you needed the
rest.
(to children)
Come on, bed! Timothy, bed!
(Timothy is banging even louder around PRO-
FESSOR JOHNS*)*
Stop banging! Come on, say goodnight to Alex.

ALEX bends to kiss CHILDREN. The SMALL CHILDREN go,
under LUCY's charge.

ALEX
(to ALVA*)*
I'm so sorry about Kenyatta.

ALVA
It must have been awful for you.

ALEX
For *us?*

Pause.

ALEX
Where's Bob?

SUNDAY

ALVA

(stiffly)
He's upstairs with his mates.
Working. In the middle of your weekend.

ALEX looks apologetic.

HODSONS' PLAYROOM.

TONY and his girl, RENEE, are sitting on a climbing tree. TOMMY is talking to BOB. PIP, TOMMY's girl, is parked in an armchair with a tonic water. RENEE also has a tonic water and never moves. RENEE and PIP are the true contemporary birds. Silent, long-haired, groomed, beautiful, and entirely without expression. They might be impassive, or simply bored. The harmonograph is being gently handed from BOB to TOMMY while they talk about how to suspend it. ALEX is sitting on a rocking-horse close to BOB: an old merry-go-round horse, with her hanging onto the stem.

BOB

Yuh, O.K., that's beautiful, but we've still got to work out how to hang it.

BOB holds up the harmonograph so that it starts to make drawings.

TONY

Still can't see why it can't be on adjustable legs.

BOB

(to ALEX)
Look, suppose you were an American business-man. Would you sooner it was on adjustable legs where anyone might bash into it but where you could move it, or would you sooner it was on the wall?

ALEX holds up the harmonograph, first free-standing, and then against the wall.

67

SUNDAY

ALEX

(choosing the wall)
Like this.
(to BOB*)*
It's worked, hasn't it?
(very pleased—with him. Shit ALVA's *piety)*
Tommy, anything against it?

BOB

He's found there'd be some manufacturing problems but I've always thought we'd do better to sell
this one outright. You know English delivery dates.

TONY

(from climbing tree)
If I were an executive, I'd want it on the wall.

TOMMY

It'll be the New York equivalent of worry beads.

Shot of harmonograph quietly making spirals. Tommy's
voice continues over.

Executives don't like playing with pens all their
lives. This is calming. That's why they like fooling
around with lawn mowers at the weekends, and
roses.

BOB

(to ALEX*)*
What do you think?

ALEX

(slowly, looking at it)
If I were a businessman, I'd think it was very beau-
tifully made.

Glance between them. Interruptions: ALVA yelling "Grub
up," BILL yelling "Come on, you lot, nosh."

SUNDAY

ALEX'S CAR. DRIVING BETWEEN GREENWICH AND HER PLACE THAT NIGHT.

BOB holds the back of ALEX's neck as she drives. She takes it for granted that they are going back to her place. Pause. She suddenly laughs. The music from "Così" is playing over.

> BOB
>
> What is it?

> ALEX
>
> This weekend *alone* together—we've never seen less of one another.

> BOB
>
> Yuh.

Pause.

> BOB
>
> *(nicely)*
> Thanks.

Traffic lights. BOB, hand on car door handle, starts to lean towards her to kiss her.

> BOB
>
> Let me off here, love. I can get a cab.

> ALEX
> *(shocked, concealing it too late)*
> Aren't you coming home?

BOB kisses her on the neck.

> BOB
>
> Got to get me eight hours.

69

SUNDAY

He whistles a taxi from the open window of the car and gets it to stop. The sort of operation that other people bungle.

ALEX'S STUDIO. SAME NIGHT.

ALEX comes into the room as she left it on Friday night. The spilt ashtray; the newspapers and books on the bed; the remains of the coffee-making in the kitchen.

MONDAY

BOB'S PAD. MONDAY MORNING.

BOB's phone rings over the cut. The title "MONDAY" is on the frame. Circular track around his desk, seen through a jumble of half-finished projects. The phone is ringing from the middle of his desk. Out of focus, we see his heaving body waking up under his Indian blanket. In focus, he leans out of bed and picks up the telephone.

> BOB
> *(on telephone, very sleepy to start with)*
> No, I was just up working till very late . . . Oh, shit. But I thought they'd made up their minds about it . . . Completely caput, or are they still interested? . . . Well, screw it, we'll write it off. What happened about the . . .
> *(picking up pace)*
> Would we get a better deal in Dallas? . . . Well, all right, see you.

He puts the receiver down and shoves a pillow over his head to shut out the light.

ALEX'S PARENTS' DINING ROOM. MONDAY NIGHT.

ALEX is halfway through dinner with her PARENTS, who

71

sit at either end of a long walnut table. There is a DOG half-visible at her feet.

MR. and MRS. GREVILLE are inconspicuously upper class. MRS. GREVILLE is wearing an old cardigan over a crepe dress. A MAID comes in and goes first to MRS. GREVILLE with a pudding dish nearly empty.

ALEX

Second helps.

Glance of family code between herself and her FATHER. MRS. GREVILLE refuses. The MAID goes to ALEX, who takes half of what's left of the pudding. MR. GREVILLE takes practically nothing. The telephone outside rings.

MR. GREVILLE

That'll be New York again.

MR. GREVILLE goes out. ALEX looks at his remnant of pudding.

MRS. GREVILLE

(to ALEX)
We might as well have some port together, then, as there aren't any men to leave to it.

MR. GREVILLE'S STUDY. MONDAY NIGHT.

Telephone ringing.

MR. GREVILLE is on the telephone to New York.

On his right is a tickertape machine carrying share and commodity prices: tin, gold, lead, copper, sugar, pepper from all over the world.

On his left is a comptometer for working out yields.

ALEX comes in with coffee and sugar on a silver tray. She tries to attract his attention.

72

MONDAY

MR. GREVILLE shoos her away, continuing his conversation.

GREVILLE DINING ROOM. MONDAY NIGHT.

MRS. GREVILLE is at the far end of the dining room.

A MAID takes away the pudding plates.

ALEX comes in.

> ALEX
> What's all the stuff to Wall Street about?

> MRS. GREVILLE
> Bank rate.

ALEX makes a tired sound.

> MRS. GREVILLE
> No, he's in fine form.
> *(grinning to herself)*
> I haven't seen him so spry since the General Strike.

> ALEX
> When he was a smart undergraduate, strike-breaking.

> MRS. GREVILLE
> Before you were born. Should you talk about what you don't know about?

> ALEX
> O.K. But you agreed with him, yes?

> MRS. GREVILLE
> I didn't, as it happened. But we were very young. I didn't think it would matter.

> ALEX
> Well, it hasn't mattered, has it?
> *(sharp)*

MONDAY

The marriage has lasted.
(long silence)

SERVANT comes in with a silver tray of coffee and a
science-fiction book on the tray. She puts it in front of
MRS. GREVILLE.

ALEX
I wish you didn't have David to dine here.

MRS. GREVILLE
He wants you back, you know.

ALEX
(shakes head)
Please.

MRS. GREVILLE
Daddy and I are fond of him.

ALEX
Look, I don't want to talk about it.

MRS. GREVILLE
He feels very bitterly about your having taken the
books.

ALEX
They were mine. They were all I took.

MRS. GREVILLE
They leave gaps, he says.

ALEX
Oh Jesus. Does being married ever come down to
anything but property, ever?

MRS. GREVILLE
Sometimes.
*(she looks at the book she would like to be
reading)*

ALEX looks at her. Sympathy. That sounded sad.

> ALEX
> What's the book tonight?
> *(friendly. Quite tender)*
> Town Planning in 1580?

MRS. GREVILLE holds up a pulp science-fiction book.

> ALEX
> Good lord.

> MRS. GREVILLE
> I know it looks lurid, but it's rather interesting.

> ALEX
> No, I didn't mean that.
> *(pause)*
> You see too little of people.

> MRS. GREVILLE
> Enough.

> ALEX
> I mean too little of Daddy.

MRS. GREVILLE makes a movement brushing the idea away.

> MRS. GREVILLE
> Well, it's not much use to start wanting things of him.
> *(pause)*
> Though I'm not always very good at stopping myself.

> ALEX
> *(looking at her carefully)*
> What? *You?*

MRS. GREVILLE looks away. The telephone outside goes again. MRS. GREVILLE pours herself more coffee.

ALEX
Well, I wish you didn't have to put up with it. But why do you?

A telephone rings again.

ALEX
The other line, naturally.

MRS. GREVILLE
He's busy. It's a heavy week.

ALEX
Oh, stop protecting him. It's *always* a heavy week.

MRS. GREVILLE
You complain about your father. Perhaps you're complaining about whoever it is you see.

ALEX plays with the RETRIEVER under the table with her feet.

MRS. GREVILLE
Are you in trouble?

ALEX shrugs.

MRS. GREVILLE
Who *are* you seeing now?

ALEX
(gets up)
Same person. On and off.

MRS. GREVILLE
On and off. You're not giving it a chance.

76

MONDAY

ALEX

I can't see why having an affair with someone on and off is any worse than being married for a course or two at mealtimes.
(pause)

MRS. GREVILLE gets up and goes to the sideboard. She finds some dinner mints.

MRS. GREVILLE

What sort of man is he?

ALEX

I don't think you'd like his haircut.

MRS. GREVILLE

Is he a hippie? But I *like* hippies.
(to herself)
They hate business and competitiveness. I think that's what's always attracted me to them.

ALEX

(rudely)
What, you?
(pause)
I'm sorry. I'm sorry. I'm sorry.

MRS. GREVILLE stands near her daughter and hands her a mint.

MRS. GREVILLE

Darling, you keep throwing in your hand because you haven't got the whole thing.
(pause)
There *is* no whole thing. One has to make it work.

Close-up on ALEX's face. Startled and moved. Waiting to hear the rest. MRS. GREVILLE hesitates and then goes on. An offering.

MONDAY

MRS. GREVILLE

What you don't know is that there was a time when
I left him. We had different opinions about everything. *Everything* seemed impossible.

ALEX

When?

MRS. GREVILLE

You were three. He left me alone. It was good of
him.
    (pause)
But I was mad not to know how much I was going
to miss him.

MRS. GREVILLE moves to the door. The RETRIEVER gets
up and follows her and then pads out, preceding her.
She pauses with her hand on the handle and then looks
back at ALEX.

MRS. GREVILLE

You think it's nothing, but it's not nothing.

ALEX watches her MOTHER leave. Shot shows MRS.
GREVILLE wavering at her HUSBAND's door and then
leaving it, hearing him on the telephone. She is used
to that particular disappointment by now. She goes down
a long corridor. Sound of adding machine over.

GREVILLE BLOCK OF FLATS. NIGHT.

ALEX clangs shut the doors of the lift and walks down
the long ground-floor passage.

ALEX DRIVING HOME AT NIGHT.

Briefly recap section of ALEX gas-mask dream sequence:
FATHER bicycling away.

LONDON CRESCENT WHERE BOB LIVES. NIGHT.

ALEX compulsively drives home the long way round so that she can have a look up at BOB's pad. After a while, another shot establishes that DANIEL in his car is doing the same thing. At one point they pass one another. Both have slowed down as they passed the window, but not stopped. They don't notice one another. BOB's pad has a psychedelic window-box. Within, from DANIEL's and ALEX's point-of-view, we see only the horned buffalo head on the white wall.

TUESDAY

ALEX'S STUDIO AND THE ANSWERING SER-
VICE.

ALEX is at her desk, on the telephone to the ANSWERING
SERVICE. "TUESDAY" title on frame.

> ANSWERING SERVICE
> Nothing for you, Miss Greville.

> ALEX
> *(to rob the woman of that small triumph)*
> Well, that's a relief.

> ANSWERING SERVICE
> *(severely)*
> Will you be picking up now?

> ALEX
> No. I'm going to bed. I'm only in if Mr. Elkin rings.
> Tell him to ring twice so I'll know it's him . . .
> *(starts to ring off)*

> ANSWERING SERVICE
> *(silkily)*
> Miss Greville, have you by any chance tried him at
> 730–1624? He's often there.

81

TUESDAY

ALEX

I wouldn't want to ring him at that number. It's a
doctor, you see.

ANSWERING SERVICE

I know that. It's Dr. Hirsh. Dr. Hirsh also uses this
service.

ALEX raises eyebrows.

ALEX

Right.

WEDNESDAY

ALEX'S STUDIO. DAY.

Shot of morning light coming in through Swedish net
curtains. "WEDNESDAY" title on shot. The telephone
goes, stops, and then goes again. Eventual track round
to ALEX in bed, who picks it up.

> ALEX
> Hallo, my duck. No, I just haven't had coffee yet . . .

> BOB
> *(on telephone)*
> It makes you sound like Lauren Bacall.

> ALEX
> That's nice. Are you alone?

> BOB
> *(on telephone)*
> Yuh, apart from the toucan.

ALEX'S IMAGINATION SCENE IN HER STUDIO,
STRAIGHT ON IN TIME.

ALEX in bed with BOB, continuing conversation, lying
very close together.

WEDNESDAY

ALEX

Are we going to see each other tonight?

BOB

I can't, darling.
(touches her hair)

ALEX

I'm going to get my hair cut.

BOB

If you take too much off I'll wallop you.

ALEX'S STUDIO, REALITY, STRAIGHT ON IN TIME.

ALEX now alone on phone.

ALEX

I'll see.

BOB

Is it all right about tonight?

ALEX

Yes, flower, of course it's all right. As always.

BOB

I don't think I can do tomorrow either. I've got to work.

ANSWERING SERVICE.

The WOMAN, with earphones, listens to their conversation.

ALEX'S STUDIO.

ALEX in bed, on telephone alone.

ALEX

Yuh, well, I might not be able to do tomorrow myself.

(she turns over)

That's fine. Maybe the night after.

CLOSE-UP OF ALEX'S FACE IN HAIR-DRESSING MIRROR.

Looking at her wet hair. Scissors snip off a couple of inches neatly on each side of her face and the locks fall to the floor.

Pull back revealing ALEX at the hairdresser's.

TIME-JUMP TO SHOT OF HER UNDER THE DRYER.

The other WOMEN are reading magazines and have their legs up on stools. ALEX has her legs down. Some of the WOMEN have fallen asleep under the dryer, but she is wide awake planning her letter of resignation. She looks in her bag for something to write on and eventually scribbles on the back of a cheque.

ALEX (voice over)

Dear Reggie, I dare say you won't be surprised that I want to quit. I'd like to do it next week. There's no point in going into it, is there? Though I will if you want. I've no stomach for the work, that's all. Sorry about it.

ALEX'S OFFICE.

The usual new enlightened building, like a glass egg-box. PEOPLE come streaming along the corridors, which are scarcely more than aisles, since no one has more than a chin-high glass partition for office walls. PEOPLE still knock on these partitions, as though there were privacy in them, and put their heads round to say "Good night." The office empties. ALEX is left talking to a BUSINESS-MAN who is at the end of his tether.

WEDNESDAY

ALEX

You've gone and made a shambles of it, haven't you?

(pause)

This place might be all right if it had any walls.

BUSINESSMAN

It's my age, isn't it? That's all there is to it. If you're near fifty-five, in a properly run business, you go over the hump—

ALEX

(over him)

You shouldn't say "gone over the hump" about yourself.

BUSINESSMAN

—and you get the golden handshake or a sherry party, and you can't find another job, and that's that.

ALEX

You'd have got this job we found you if only you hadn't invented that degree. Why did you do it? An *engineering* degree.

BUSINESSMAN

There's no point in going on at me.

ALEX

You'd been accepted and then you had to go and muck it up.

BUSINESSMAN

How am I going to tell my wife?

ALEX

Why come here if you won't let us help you?

WEDNESDAY

BUSINESSMAN

You? It's firms like you that are putting me out to grass. Me and the other fifty-three-year-olds.

ALEX

You told me fifty-five.

BUSINESSMAN

(stubborn)
Fifty-three.

ALEX

(lightly, trying to lift the mood, knowing he's lying)
Hang on to that, then.
(pause. The office overhead lights go off during the last sentence)
Would you have liked to have done engineering?
(pause)

BUSINESSMAN

You're an attractive girl.

ALEX

(fobbing him off)
You've messed this chance up and I don't know if we'll be able to fix another.
(head on hands)
I'm so sorry.
(pause)
They'll take up references.
(she starts to wipe her eyes)

BUSINESSMAN

Don't you start.

ALEX looks at him with great concern. He jousts vaguely with his arms, looking for a target.

She gives him a cigarette.

87

> BUSINESSMAN
> *(trying to recover)*
> Well, is there anything you can do or not? Are you an expert or not? I've been behind a desk twice the size of that for thirty years. I've had three secretaries at a time.

> ALEX
> If it's any comfort to you, I won't be here after next week. I'm packing it in.

> BUSINESSMAN
> Then who'm I supposed to deal with?

SAME OFFICE SCENE. DARKER OUTSIDE.

Lights have been going off at the far end of the office floor. The last PERSON in shouts "Good night" and waves. The BUSINESSMAN is holding ALEX's hand. They have been drinking whisky. Glasses and a bottle on her desk.

> ALEX
> *(peering at him in her way)*
> Are you really all right?

> BUSINESSMAN
> Face-lift's gone, that's what you're seeing.

ALEX lets go of his hand in recoil, regrets that instantly, and watches him, sick for him.

> BUSINESSMAN
> *(truculent)*
> Didn't you know that?

She gives him a whisky.

> BUSINESSMAN
> You're the only girl I've ever met who kept booze in her desk. We can get our faces done, you know.

For interviews. They told me down the corridor. It lasts two days. They stretch the skin. I surprised myself. I looked forty-two. I didn't go home.
(uneasy)
My wife might have been upset. We're all right, you see. I don't know how to tell her.

ALEX
You mean you haven't told her about the *sack?*

She has pushed her hair back in amazement on this line and then pulled back the skin a little on each side of her eyes.

BUSINESSMAN
(fascinated)
Yes, like that.

He does it to himself, just enough to brace the skin, and gives her a grotesque cheered-up grin. His new confidence is rather upsetting.

BUSINESSMAN
How about some dinner?

OFFICE CLOAKROOM.

ALEX is in front of the mirror, not looking at her reflection but at her hands, moving the fingers up and down, stretching the skin, pulling it back from her knuckles to her wrist. Already it makes a difference and she is only thirty-four.

DANIEL'S LIBRARY. NIGHT.

DANIEL is having a party. BOB is there and four other MEN. Two of them have young WIVES whom they have brought. There is also a WOMAN of about fifty-five, a White Russian emigrée, who has known DANIEL and BOB a long time. They are playing The Game. Atmosphere of intimacy and a good evening. DANIEL is doing a brilliant rapid mime of "Great Expectations" or "The Greatest Story Ever Told." BOB and the RUSSIAN WOMAN keep guessing right very fast; and BOB, laughing, pours drinks in the middle of guessing, his eyes on DANIEL. The cuts concentrate on DANIEL's hand movements.

ALEX'S STUDIO, SIMULTANEOUS TIME.

Cuts of more hands, as in the last scene. But lovers' hands, this time. The BUSINESSMAN is in bed with ALEX. "Così" continues over this and changes over the next cut into the sound of DANIEL's doorbell.

DANIEL'S HOUSE, STRAIGHT ON IN TIME.

The doorbell has just finished ringing. We pick up the sound of The Game being played. BOB runs cheerfully to the door and opens it, still in the mood of the party. A MAN whom he knows and doesn't much like is standing outside with his head turned round to a row going on in the parked car he has just left. A MARRIED WOMAN is sitting in the front passenger seat, facing forward stonily. The car door is open and she is refusing to get out. Her HUSBAND is walking away from the car down the street, throwing his hands up, speechless. The QUEER FRIEND of the MAN on the doorstep is lounging against the area railings, watching the spectacle.

BOB

What's going on?

MAN ON DOORSTEP

Hi.

WIFE
(shouts at HUSBAND*)*
Journalistic hack.

He continues walking away from her, shouting, without turning.

90

WEDNESDAY

HUSBAND

You'd better start getting up in the morning.

MAN ON DOORSTEP
(to BOB*)*
They've been going on like this all evening.

WIFE

Where's my manuscript?

HUSBAND
(starts walking back to her, fast)
You bitch. What put that into your head? Have
you been at my desk?

MAN ON DOORSTEP
(yells at them)
Oh, do shut up and come in.

WIFE
(not budging, spitting the line out to her
HUSBAND*)*
Reporter! Newspaperman!

HUSBAND

I'm going in and you're bloody coming too.

He starts dragging her by the arm. BOB lightly loathes it
all. The brawling COUPLE pass him on the doorstep and
continue down the passage.

WIFE

I know you took my manuscript.

HUSBAND

It's only a cookery book, for Christ's sake.

WIFE

At least it's a *book*.

WEDNESDAY

HUSBAND

You're intolerable when you're smashed.

MAN'S FRIEND
(to BOB *as he passes him)*
It's like a bad bullfight, dear.

Shot of front door closing from the inside.

DANIEL'S PARTY.

The row is still going on. The mood of the first part of
the evening has been destroyed. The original GUESTS are
trying to keep going, ignoring the fight as much as possible, smiling. Smoking. DANIEL has a bottle of brandy
in his hand. BOB is standing near him. They both watch
the fighting COUPLE, who are by the fireplace.

WIFE
You'd never have driven here that stupid way if
you hadn't had her on your mind.

HUSBAND

Who's "her"?

WIFE
(laughs at him)
Coming through Pelham Crescent!

DANIEL moves up to them.

HUSBAND
What's so special about coming through Pelham
Crescent?

WIFE
Exactly. That's what I mean. If you hadn't been
feeling guilty, you'd have gone along the Fulham
Road.

Sarcastic applause from the QUEENS and theatrical yawns.

92

WEDNESDAY

DANIEL

For Christ's sake, stop it.

He puts his hands on both of them, trying to force a gap. The WOMAN slaps his hand and wheels on him.

WIFE

Daniel, get lost, will you? You don't know a thing about it.

QUEENS' VOICES
(from sofa, almost simultaneous)
Oh leave it, dear, leave them be. She *will* do it when she's pissed.

Shot of DANIEL withdrawing. At a loss, slightly humiliated and angry.

The row continues as he makes his way to BOB, who has successfully closed his ears to the fight and is sitting behind DANIEL's desk opening and shutting drawers.

WIFE

I am *not* pissed.

HUSBAND

And what about *Uncle* Keith, and *Uncle* David, and *Uncle all the rest,* then? In front of the children.

WIFE

Don't be pious. What about your *saying* "Uncle" in front of the children?

HUSBAND

Pelham Crescent is a perfectly normal way to come.

WIFE starts to take off her shirt.

WEDNESDAY

HUSBAND

Oh, Jesus, now she's taking off her shirt. Somebody stop her.

MAN'S FRIEND

She's your wife, darling.

DANIEL
(to BOB, *low voice under fight. Riled)*
What's the matter with *you?*

BOB

Nothing. They're ridiculous, that's all.

BOB finds a stamp and puts it on an envelope that he has taken out of his hip pocket. Unperturbed.

DANIEL

You might help.

HUSBAND
(to room, over)
Once she starts, she doesn't stop.

MAN FROM DOORSTEP

Somebody cart the lovely carcass up to bed. She's pissed.

WIFE

I am *not* pissed, I tell you.
(she takes off her shirt)

There are yells of "Shut up" and responses to the sound of someone having broken a glass. General hubbub. BOB gets up. DANIEL goes quickly after him, grabbing his arm.

STAIRS AND LANDING FROM DANIEL'S LIBRARY.

BOB goes towards stairs, DANIEL follows.

WEDNESDAY

DANIEL

What's the matter?

BOB

I'm going.

DANIEL

For Christ's sake!

BOB

I've got to.

DANIEL

Well, go upstairs. I'll get rid of them. I'll come up as soon as I can.

BOB

Sorry.

DANIEL

Thanks for the support.

BOB

They're your friends.

DANIEL

I don't like them when they're like this any more than you do.

BOB

Then why see them?

DANIEL

I've known them for ten years. I didn't *ask* them tonight. You didn't exactly bang the door.

BOB AND DANIEL ARE NOW ON THE DOOR-STEP.

BOB

I said I'm sorry. I'd just rather be on my own.

WEDNESDAY

DANIEL blazes.

> DANIEL
> That's *fine*.

> BOB
> I just can't stand people carrying on.

> DANIEL
> —O.K. Off.

The shot goes with BOB, walking along with his hands in his pockets. He disappears.

DANIEL'S LIBRARY.

The WIFE is being forcibly dressed by her HUSBAND. Fragmented images of the party: struggling arms, a MAN's hands doing up a WOMAN's shirt buttons, cigarettes stubbed out, drinks being poured.

> DANIEL
> *(to room, standing at door)*
> Right. That's enough. Goodnight and fuck off, the whole lot of you. Get out of my house.

BOB'S PAD.

BOB is back and in bed. He tries to sleep.

ALEX'S STUDIO. HALF AN HOUR LATER.

The BUSINESSMAN and ALEX are asleep on ALEX's bed. The telephone rings and they both wake. She goes towards the kitchen to pick it up, having difficulty rousing herself.

Electronic signals. A brief repeat of the earlier electronic image of telephone ringing. The signals and the screen go blank as the ANSWERING SERVICE picks up the call.

WEDNESDAY

ANSWERING SERVICE.

> ANSWERING SERVICE WOMAN
> Very well. I'll tell her.
> *(unplugs wires and sits back)*

ALEX'S KITCHEN. NIGHT.

She picks up the receiver and says hello.

Dead telephone, as the ANSWERING SERVICE has finished. So she starts to dial the service, her hand cupped over the receiver.

ANSWERING SERVICE. SAME TIME.

> ANSWERING SERVICE
> Miss Greville, Mr. Elkin rang. I said I thought you were in but not picking up.

> ALEX
> Charming.
> *(pause)*
> Well? What did he say?

> ANSWERING SERVICE
> *(after a pause, with triumph about delaying the message)*
> He said could he come right away?

The WOMAN goes on knitting. The ANSWERING SERVICE is a little room with a gas ring, kettle, Nescafé, piles of housekeeping magazines. A pleasant WOMAN, wearing boots.

ALEX'S STUDIO. TEN MINUTES LATER.

ALEX in a jumpsuit is tidying the fur rug on the bed and plumping the cushions.

The BUSINESSMAN is straightening his tie and bending down to look at her books on top of her gallery. ALEX

97

runs up the spiral staircase with a brandy for both of them. Then she hears BOB using his key. Through the following scenes she looks amused about her situation, and a bit amused too about the way BOB responds to it.

BOB comes into the studio and ALEX runs down the stairs and gives him a kiss. He suspects at once that they are not alone, from the way she does it perhaps. He takes in the two glasses by the bed and looks up at the gallery. ALEX shouts upstairs.

> ALEX
>
> George, come down.

She moves a few steps towards the gallery in his direction while BOB stands stock-still. The BUSINESSMAN comes down rather slowly and she finds herself making an introduction across great distances.

Wide shot of three figures, rather small, as she introduces them.

> ALEX
>
> George, this is Bob Elkin—George Harding.

BOB and the BUSINESSMAN shake hands cordially.

> BOB
>
> How do you do?

> ALEX
>
> *(to* BOB*)*
> Do you want a drink?

BOB goes to the drinks table and starts to mix himself a whisky and soda, using what he regards as his own home with perfect pleasantness but a faint edge. He sees that she hasn't got any soda and goes into the kitchen to rummage in the fridge.

> BUSINESSMAN
>
> I must be going.

98

WEDNESDAY

ALEX

Oh, no. Not yet.

BUSINESSMAN

I must catch my train.

ALEX

Thank you for dinner. Thank you.

She shakes hands with him, then kisses him, under
BOB's eye from the kitchen.

ALEX

We'll see each other next week.

BUSINESSMAN

Yes.

ALEX

Will you telephone?

The BUSINESSMAN picks up BOB's coat by mistake because it happens to be hiding his own. ALEX sees what
he is doing and, almost at the same time, grabs the coat
back from him and throws it onto another chair.

ALEX

Sorry.

BUSINESSMAN

You won't be at the office.

ALEX

Next week I will. After that, here.

ALEX follows the BUSINESSMAN to the door.

BUSINESSMAN

(at door)
Goodbye.

99

WEDNESDAY

ALEX

Thanks again.

BUSINESSMAN

Goodbye.

During this conversation they go out of the front door and down the stairs together.

BOB is left alone for a moment, looking unhappy and despondent. Unreasonably, he knows.

ALEX reappears and bends down to straighten a carpet that the front door has been sticking on, to hide that she is giggling.

BOB is at the fireplace with his back to her. He kicks the grate.

BOB

Does this thing ever work?

ALEX

Should do. It's bloody cold, isn't it?

BOB cranes his neck up the flue. ALEX walks towards the kitchen.

ALEX

I haven't got any logs. I've got a cupboard I can burn.

She reappears after a moment with an armful of old shelves and cardboard boxes, and starts to make a fire in the grate.

ALEX

I am glad you came. It's nice to see you.

BOB

(*picks up his thrown coat from the sofa and rehangs it rebukingly over the sofa back*)
It looked as if I was interrupting.

100

WEDNESDAY

ALEX

You're not miffed, are you?

BOB

Not a bit.
    (dignified)
I suppose I thought you'd be alone at this hour.

ALEX

Well, we're alone now.
    (pause)
Stop looking desolate.

BOB

You've had your hair cut.

ALEX

Yuh.

BOB

Doesn't look as bad as I thought.

ALEX goes on looking at the fire she has made.

ALEX

It still won't last more than ten minutes. There's some damp stuff we could get from the roof to stop it burning so fast.

ALEX'S ROOF. NIGHT.

The two of them together in the dark on the flat roof. Chimney stacks: wide perspective.

They hunt for bits of sticks and boxes, making a pile to carry down the fire-escape stairs. A jet flies over, making an unnaturally loud noise. ALEX watches the jet zoom away.

ALEX

Too low, isn't it?

BOB

Well, I suppose we'll either hear the crash or read the headlines.

ALEX'S STUDIO. NIGHT.

The two of them are lying naked in front of the fire.

THURSDAY

ALEX'S STUDIO. NEXT MORNING.

A bitterly cold dawn. The plants outside the window look grey. BOB and ALEX, naked, go towards the bed from the fireplace where they have just woken up. The title "THURSDAY" is on the shot. There is a terrific racket from a building site nearby. ALEX and BOB lie together in bed. She is on her back with her eyes closed. He is on his side looking at her with half opened eyes. A long beat.

> BOB
> Who was that guy last night?

> ALEX
> I told you. His name's George.

> BOB
> Who is he?

> ALEX
> He's a man from the office and he's lost his job and I'm trying to find him another one.
> *(pause.* ALEX *is still flat on her back with her eyes closed)*
> Do you mind about him?

103

THURSDAY

BOB

No.

ALEX

(turns round to look at him)
You really *don't* mind that, do you?

BOB shakes his head.

BOB

No. Not a bit. We're free to do what we want.

ALEX

Darling.
(she gets up on her elbow and shakes her head, looking down at him)
Look. Other people often do what they don't want to do at all.

Pause.

ITALIAN STATE TOURIST OFFICE. DAY.

Tracking past a poster in the window of the Tourist Office, traffic and passersby reflected, we pick up DANIEL and a WOMAN CLERK at counter inside. DANIEL, his well-worn map of Italy spread out on the desk, sketches his route with crosses and lines as he talks.

DANIEL

. . . then we're going from Bellagio and the Lakes on to Ravenna—and then—

CLERK

(interrupting him as she slams down brochures)
Bellagio and the Lakes. Mountains. Boat trips. Views.
(she slams down a brochure for each)
Ravenna. Churches. Hotels. Tours.
(she slams down brochures)

THURSDAY

DANIEL

Thank you—and then through down to Tuscany—
here, to Siena.
(makes a cross)

CLERK
(slamming down brochures)
Siena. Churches. Museums. Hotels.

DANIEL

Tell me—I've been told about a very good hotel
between Siena and Florence. Somewhere here.
Do you happen to know it?

CLERK

Yes.

DANIEL

Can you recommend it?

CLERK

I'm sorry. We're not allowed to recommend spe-
cific hotels. This is a State Tourist Bureau.

DANIEL

But that's ridiculous—since you've been there and
know the place.

CLERK

I've given you the official list—

DANIEL
(interrupting)
Look—couldn't for once the Italian State Tourist
Bureau be persuaded to break a rule? . . .

CLERK
(with pomp)
I'm sorry . . .

105

THURSDAY

DANIEL

Just whisper.
(whispering)
Is it terrible?

CLERK
(relenting, whispers back)
No, it's very good.

T.W.A. TERMINAL. DAY.

BOB goes towards the entrance and inside, passing people. One AMERICAN BUSINESSMAN is saying goodbye to another. Another AMERICAN is asking about the rate of exchange at the bank counter.

T.W.A. TERMINAL SURGERY.

BOB is with T.W.A. DOCTOR, an elderly and gentle Scotsman.

BOB
I just need a smallpox injection.

DOCTOR
Boost?

BOB
What?

DOCTOR
When was the last?

BOB
When I was born, I should think.

Officialdom with paperwork and serum.

DOCTOR
Going to America?

106

THURSDAY

BOB

Maybe.

DOCTOR

You must go to San Francisco. That's a lovely place.

FRIDAY

INTERIOR OF BAR AND RESTAURANT.

The title "FRIDAY" is on the frame.

DANIEL is sitting alone at the bar portion of a restaurant eating nuts and olives and finishing a whisky sour. He is studying the brochures from the Tourist Bureau.

The WAITER comes up to him with a menu and asks him if he wants to order.

DANIEL takes the menu and the WAITER goes off to answer the telephone.

He comes back towards DANIEL.

> WAITER
> Dr. Hirsh, Mr. Elkin has just rung and says he's sorry, but he doesn't feel well and won't be joining you.

BOB'S PAD. NIGHT.

DANIEL, with overcoat still on, is shining a torch down BOB's throat.

> DANIEL
> Why the hell didn't you say you were ill? Instead of just not turning up as usual?

FRIDAY

BOB

Are you still going on at me about Wednesday night?

DANIEL

No, of course not. Say ah. That looks O.K. What have you been eating?

BOB

I don't think it's that.

DANIEL

Well, you've got a temperature all right.

BOB
(sending him up)
Now tell me to take some aspirin.

DANIEL
(picking up the note; an old routine between them)
Yes, take plenty of aspirin.

BOB

And fluids.

DANIEL

And fluids.
(pause. Change of voice)
I got the bumph about taking the car to Nice.

BOB shivers.

DANIEL
(showing BOB a brochure)
Your temperature's going up.

DANIEL leans over BOB, against the vaccinated arm, and BOB jumps a mile.

Close-up of DANIEL's face.

FRIDAY

> BOB

Oh, shit, I'll have to tell you. I had a vaccination yesterday. For smallpox.

> DANIEL

Why the hell didn't you come to me?

> BOB

I just thought—I didn't want—

> DANIEL
> *(after a pause)*

That means America.

> BOB

I think.
> *(pause)*

Not for long.

DANIEL throws the brochures and some tickets into a wastepaper basket.

> DANIEL

I always knew Italy was a fiction.

BOB gets up and rescues the papers.

> BOB

Hey, don't do that. We'll go when I get back.
> *(pause)*

I want to, a lot.

> DANIEL
> *(glaring. Wretched underneath)*

It's pointless.

> BOB

Do you want a drink?

> DANIEL

No.

They are both standing. DANIEL turns away and makes himself say the next thing.

> DANIEL
>
> America would be for much longer than you say, wouldn't it?

> BOB
>
> I don't know. I'll have to play it by ear when I get there.

> DANIEL
>
> Do you like the people there?

> BOB
>
> I don't know many. It's a chance.
> *(pause)*
> I don't have to go. I could send Tony.

> DANIEL
>
> Well, that's got to be your choice.

> BOB
>
> *(half over him, refusing to accept the responsibility)*
> I couldn't ever just piss off, you see.

Cut to close-up of DANIEL's face, raising eyebrows, registering sadly that BOB could almost certainly do just that. And indeed we have just seen him trying to.

> DANIEL
>
> Have you told Alex?

> BOB
>
> No.

> DANIEL
>
> Why not?

FRIDAY

BOB

I don't know what to do. Should I go? What do
you think?

DANIEL

I told you, you've got to decide. I can see it might
solve a lot of problems for you if you went.
(pause)
But.

Hold on DANIEL's face looking at BOB.

Cut to BOB's face avoiding that, lighting a cigarette.

SATURDAY

THE INSIDE OF THE FAMILY SYNAGOGUE
WITH THE HIRSHES.

The title "SATURDAY" is on the frame.

DANIEL is coming down the aisle. On his way he is
greeted by one or two ACQUAINTANCES with nods and
smiles.

He reaches the front row of the centre block, occupied
by MALE RELATIVES and the men of his immediate
family. The relations acknowledge him as he goes by.
He reaches an old man, his FATHER, a younger man, his
BROTHER, and on the end seat of the row a thirteen-
year-old called JONATHAN, the day's Bar Mitzvah.

Affectionate greetings in whispers.

> DANIEL
> *(low voice)*
> Hello, Father—David—Jonathan.
> *(to* JONATHAN*)*
> Good luck.

DANIEL glances up at the gallery.

His MOTHER and SISTER-IN-LAW are standing there,
looking down. They smile and give little waves of hand.

SATURDAY

Meanwhile his FATHER gets out a tallis and book from his seat-box and gives them to DANIEL.

Intercut DANIEL's reactions to the ritual, and to his family, including JONATHAN, whose head is still bent to his book, covertly rehearsing his piece. The sense of tribe is strong. It was once a support to DANIEL, up to a point, but he has relinquished most of it, or it has relinquished him.

Sound changes to CANTOR calling up JONATHAN.

DANIEL gives JONATHAN fingers-crossed sign.

Silence.

JONATHAN nervously approaches the dais.

DANIEL, FATHER, BROTHER, SISTER-IN-LAW, MOTHER all rooting for him.

DANIEL'S RECOLLECTION OF THE SAME SYN-AGOGUE IN 1930'S.

The young DANIEL completes the walk begun by JONA-THAN.

The young DANIEL is at the desk, before the open scroll. He sings the blessing.

He is flanked by his FATHER on one side, the THIRTIES CANTOR and GRANDFATHER on the other.

Before him he sees the expectant CONGREGATION.

—his MOTHER and GRANDMOTHER in the gallery, en-couraging—

—his GRANDFATHER and FATHER on either side of him, encouraging—

THIRTIES RABBI

Daniel Hirsh—

Young DANIEL listens.

SATURDAY

SYNAGOGUE, IN PRESENT TIME.

DANIEL listening to the RABBI, who is going on with his address to JONATHAN.

Mix to noise of glasses and hubbub of conversation.

THE NAPOLEON ROOM. CAFÉ ROYAL. NIGHT.

Bar Mitzvah party of DANIEL'S FAMILY, their RELATIONS and BUSINESS ASSOCIATES.

DANIEL is weaving his way through the crowd in the direction of JONATHAN. RELATIVES greet him and grasp his hand in passing.

A conjuring COUSIN is doing amateur tricks for some CHILDREN.

Meanwhile, voices over:

> WOMAN
> Your mother's cousin married a Mayer and John Mayer married Wendy Hillman, so that's how we come to be related—

> MAN
> We discussed going public but we decided it was too early—

> YOUNG MAN
> —not offhand, but come to my office on Monday and I'll look up the arrangement I made for your brother-in-law—

> YOUNG MAN
> My parents were very understanding about it, and of course I'd never do anything to hurt them—

> GIRL
> We've just come back from Israel. Daddy planted a tree—

SATURDAY

And this is my other son, Julian. He's studying
medicine. He's in his second year and doing very
well—

JONATHAN is standing lost in a small group of chatter-
ing ADULTS. DANIEL reaches him and grasps his hand
manfully.

DANIEL
Congratulations, Jonathan. You did very well.

JONATHAN
Thank you.

DANIEL'S BROTHER and SISTER-IN-LAW are nearby, talking to SELBY LOWNDES.

DANIEL
Hello, David.

BROTHER
Dan, can I introduce Selby Lowndes? My new
partner.

DANIEL
How do you do.

They shake hands.

FEMALE COUSIN, AUNT SOPHIE, and studious-looking
MARK, fourteen, appear.

DANIEL
Ah. Aunt Sophie.

AUNT SOPHIE's face, eager, remembering DANIEL in
nappies.

AUNT SOPHIE
You remember your cousin Mark.

SATURDAY

DANIEL looks at MARK, to him a total stranger.

> DANIEL
> Yes, indeed I do. Hello, Mark.

> SOPHIE
> Shake hands, Mark. Cousin Daniel knew you when you were only a baby.

They shake hands.

COUSIN ELSA bustles up, ready to devour DANIEL.

> COUSIN ELSA
> Hello, Daniel.

> DANIEL
> Hello, Elsa.

DANIEL escapes the kiss she is about to give him.

> SISTER-IN-LAW
> Now don't be fuddy-duddy today, Daniel, will you? I've put you next to an awfully nice woman. She's only just got divorced, so will you be very kind to her? I know you'll get on—

In the banqueting room, CHILDREN are rearranging their place cards.

DANIEL reaches his FATHER.

> DANIEL
> Hello, Father. Do you know all these people?

> FATHER
> No.

> DANIEL
> Quite a do.

> FATHER
> Mostly your brother's business associates.

SATURDAY

FATHER gives DANIEL a perceptive look.

>   FATHER
> How are you, son?

>   DANIEL
> I'm all right. Fine.

>   FATHER
>   *(making do with the answer)*
> Good.

DANIEL'S MOTHER bustles up with RABBI.

>   MOTHER
> This is my elder son. Rabbi Eisenberg.

>   DANIEL
> How do you do.

>   RABBI
>   *(eagerly)*
> You're Lionel, aren't you?

>   DANIEL
> No, I'm Daniel.

>   RABBI
> Of course. You're the one who's doing engineering.

>   FATHER
> No, it's medicine.

>   RABBI
> Sorry, I haven't seen you for so long.

RABBI shakes hands with DANIEL warmly, using two hands.

>   RABBI
> Nice to see you again.

SATURDAY

MOTHER takes RABBI off to meet a foreign RELATIVE, leaving DANIEL with his FATHER.

AUNT ASTRID comes up.

> AUNT ASTRID
> Oh, Daniel. How are you? You're looking very spruce.
> *(she intercepts a canapé)*
> Have one of these. Now when are *you* going to give us all a nice surprise?

FATHER's reaction: sympathetic to DANIEL.

> DANIEL
> *(expostulating)*
> Aunt Astrid!

> AUNT ASTRID
> Still holding out on us—well, it's very selfish of you—you're going to be very lonely—

> DANIEL
> I haven't found the right person yet—

ALEX'S STUDIO. SAME TIME.

BOB is hanging a clock for her. ALEX is sitting in a swivel chair. Full-face, gazing at BOB's back view on the gallery stairs.

> BOB
> Is it straight?

Silence from ALEX; BOB turns round.

> ALEX
> When are you going?

> BOB
> In a day or two.

121

SATURDAY

ALEX

(pause)
Why did I have to ask you?

Silence.

BOB

I'll be back. You'll be here. We can ring each other up.

ALEX

I'm *bound* to be here.

BOB steps back to look at the clock he has hung.

BOB

You shouldn't ever have decided to quit that job. You need something to occupy that piercing educated mind. You're at a loose end, that's all.

ALEX

No. That's absolutely not it.
(an edge in her voice that baffles BOB)

BOB

I don't get you like this—
(pause)
You could come over. Could you come over?

ALEX swivels her chair away from him.

BOB

(moving clock hands to right time)
Nothing's changed.

ALEX

(furious)
That's bang on right. That's the trouble. *Nothing's* changed. All this fitting in and shutting up and making do. Me being careful not to ask you about Daniel, Daniel not getting any answers from you

122

because you're here, my old mum not making demands for umpteen years, and my *fucking* office. I don't want us to live like this. I don't want to live like this any more. I *can't* come over. *Don't* ring. I won't be here when you come back. We've got to pack this in and I don't know what else to say.

> BOB

Look. Would it make any difference if we tried to live together? I don't want to lose you.

> ALEX

Hey. Darling. You couldn't do it. Don't even say it—
> *(tries to light cigarette)*

Blast! I've got the shakes. I bought your terms, and they were rotten terms, and I shouldn't have done it. My fault.

> BOB

You keep asking too much.

> ALEX

For God's sake. Caring about someone a lot? Is that too much? People with some time to spare for each other. Is that too much?
> (ALEX *waits until she has stopped crying*)

I've had this business that anything is better than nothing. There are times when nothing *has* to be better than anything.
> *(pause)*

If you look back on this—which you won't, my darling—you'll say it's got something to do with Daniel. It hasn't . . .

The phone goes.

BOB doesn't dare move to answer it. He watches ALEX.

ALEX answers.

> ALEX

It's New York for you. Wouldn't you know.

123

SATURDAY

BOB goes to the phone beside her bed and lies down.
ALEX begins to laugh.

> BOB
>
> Put him on.
> *(to* ALEX*)*
> What's the joke?

> ALEX
>
> I was thinking of someone else . . .

> BOB
>
> *(yelling)*
> Hi. Shout a bit, we've got a lousy connection.

> ALEX
>
> *(at the same time, softly, knowing she can't be heard)*
> . . . of my old mum, actually. You can't hear, and
> I love you a lot, and I don't want you to go.

SAVOY BALLROOM. NIGHT.

JONATHAN is on the dais. Glasses and cutlery noises.

> JONATHAN
>
> Unaccustomed as I am to public speaking, I want
> to thank my mother and father, without whom this
> speech would never have been written . . .

Laughter. Banging on tables. Applause.

> JONATHAN
>
> —for the love and the care and the devotion they
> have given to family life on this occasion when I
> feel the great weight of responsibility that lies
> ahead. I want to thank all of you for coming here
> and for the generous presents you have given me in
> these troublesome times.

124

SATURDAY

"Hear, hear." Banging on table. Loud laughter. During this speech a WAITER has gone over to DANIEL to tell him that he's wanted on the phone and he leaves.

ANSWERING SERVICE. FOLLOWING TIME.

> ANSWERING SERVICE WOMAN
> Sorry to drag you away from your party, doctor, but there's an urgent call for you to ring the R.M.O. at St. George's Hospital. That's all . . . no, and Mr. Elkin didn't call . . .

HOSPITAL BASEMENT AND STAIRS. MIDDLE OF NIGHT.

DANIEL with his case is going through the side entrance of St. George's Hospital in Grosvenor Crescent, past wheelchairs and trolleys and central heating pipes.

HOSPITAL WARD. MIDDLE OF NIGHT.

There is a light over SISTER's table. BODIES are turning restlessly in the rows of beds. Towards the end of the ward, screens are drawn round a bed. The distant figure of DANIEL, in a white coat, is in conference. The HOUSE PHYSICIAN is beside him, the SISTER respectfully near.

HOSPITAL CORRIDOR OUTSIDE THE WARD. MIDDLE OF NIGHT.

A dazed, scared COUPLE are sitting in the wide corridor on a bench with their feet together and their hands on one another's. Not demonstrative people. She has a crumpled bag of biscuits beside her and a tray of tea. DANIEL comes towards them from a ward at the other end of the corridor. The scale is immense and the human figure dwarfed. He sits beside the COUPLE and they have tea.

> WOMAN
> (to HUSBAND)
> Can you fancy a biscuit?

125

SATURDAY

HUSBAND

That doctor in the white coat said to us the race is run. He doesn't say the same as what you say.
(he breaks a biscuit, crying)
I remember the phrase because it stuck in my mind.

DANIEL

I wouldn't deceive you. I think we might have a chance.

WOMAN

He said the race is run, that's what he said.

DANIEL

I think that was earlier in the night. She's hanging on.

WOMAN

You're not thinking she'd be better gone, doctor, are you?

DANIEL

No, I'm not. I'm certainly not.

WOMAN

Doctors often say that. They have to, don't they?

DANIEL
(shakes his head)
She might make it, you see. You know that would be best.

WOMAN

If she couldn't move?

Pause.

DANIEL

People can manage on very little.

Pause.

SATURDAY

HUSBAND

Listen to him, dear. There's a chance, he's saying.

The WOMAN stares down the corridor for a long time. Overhead lights glimmer at intervals along the great length.

WOMAN

The electricity bills must be terrible.

DANIEL'S HOUSE THAT NIGHT.

DANIEL uses the key and climbs the stairs inside, switching off the lights at each landing as he goes. In his bedroom, he sees BOB in the bed and stands there watching him. Surprised. Happy. Less exhausted. He sits on the edge of the bed and takes off his tie and then his shoes, very quietly. BOB's head is half-buried under a pillow as usual.

DAYDREAM SHOT OF HOSPITAL.

DANIEL imagines that BOB is lying paralysed in a hospital bed. The bed is like the one he has just left at St. George's Hospital; it is also, horribly, his own bed at home. BOB's face is streaming with tears, and nothing will move but his eyes as the telephone rings.

DANIEL'S BEDROOM. FIRST LIGHT.

The telephone rings faintly in the hall below. DANIEL, still sitting on the bed, picks up the receiver.

DANIEL

Yes.
    (pause)
I think you'd better give her pethidine.
    (pause)
Right.

BOB is awake.

SATURDAY

DANIEL puts down the phone and goes into the bathroom.

> BOB
> It's bloody late. Was the Bar Mitzvah okay?

> DANIEL
> I've been at hospital.

> BOB
> Will he be all right?

> DANIEL
> She. She may just pull through.
> *(lets out a breath)*
> Aaah. It's much better now you're awake.

Jump cut to BOB putting his arms round DANIEL, who is getting into bed.

> BOB
> You take a lot of trouble about your family, don't you?

> DANIEL
> Are you in love with Alex?

> BOB
> I don't think so, but I can't be sure.

> DANIEL
> The truth is I don't want to lose you.

> BOB
> I'll be back sometime.

DANIEL holds BOB's face.

The image freezes.

SUNDAY

DANIEL'S CONSULTING ROOM AND GARDEN.
DAWN.

"SUNDAY" title on shot.

DANIEL is playing Italian language-records, wearing a polo-necked sweater and grey flannels. He opens the French windows.

He walks out to his pool and crouches down to look at the goldfish. The sound of the recorded voice comes out into the cold garden. Time passes.

DANIEL'S STAIRS. DAWN.

BOB is coming quietly down the stairs in a raincoat. He leaves the front door key on the kitchen table.

DANIEL is still crouched by the pool. He has his head bent and the sight of BOB going out of the house is not visible to him.

STREET OUTSIDE DANIEL'S HOUSE. DAWN.

Long shot of BOB letting himself out of DANIEL's house.

ANSWERING SERVICE. EARLY MORNING.

SUNDAY

ANSWERING SERVICE WOMAN

We'll be sorry, Mr. Elkin. But you'll be back, will
you? Well, I can't say I blame you. The dollar's
where the future is. I'll give that message to Miss
Greville, yes. And to Dr. . . . ? Well, very well.

She unplugs, and smirks a bit and nods to herself, and
opens a packet of fruit pastilles.

BOB'S PAD. SUNDAY MORNING.

He comes downstairs with rubbish and leaves it outside
his front door. A VOICE from the area yells up.

VOICE FROM AREA

Rubbish belongs down here, Mr. Elkin.

He slams the front door behind him and goes away.

THE HODSONS'. SUNDAY MORNING.

ALEX drives up in her car, looking at the HODSON FAMILY
having lunch inside the house. DANIEL is with the FAMILY
and PROFESSOR JOHNS.

ALVA

When are you off to Italy?

DANIEL

The twenty-first, God willing.

ALVA

Are you going with Bob?

DANIEL

I don't think so.

ALVA makes commiserating sound, checked by BILL.

BILL

We've always thought we should try to be a bit
more grown-up ourselves about having holidays on

130

our own. Separately, I mean. Have you ever thought of one of those Scholars' Cruises? Alva nearly went on one.

DANIEL

It isn't what I'd have chosen.

ALVA makes her own married warning gesture to BILL and speaks to DANIEL, meaning what she says, in her own way.

ALVA

I'm terribly sorry.

Sprightly snigger from LUCY. DANIEL looks at them coldly.

DANIEL

No need.

There is a view of the scene from the outside of the house, from ALEX's point of view, and a long snatch of "Così." DANIEL comes out of the house.

ALEX gets out of her car and sits on the wing of his. They shake hands, absurdly. He sits down in his own driving seat.

ALEX

I didn't know you were going to be here. I'm sorry. You know who I am.

DANIEL

Thank you for not coming in. You must have been out here a long time.
  (awkward)
Have you had lunch?

ALEX

It's the sort of thing we say, isn't it?
  (pause)

131

I'm ravenous.
    (pause)
He's all right, is he?

DANIEL

I think so.
    (pause)
This isn't very easy, is it?

She shakes her head.

ALEX

I thought he'd be with you today.

They light cigarettes.

DANIEL

He's gone away, yes?

ALEX

I don't know.

DANIEL

It's all right to tell me.

ALEX

I'm sorry. I only had it from the answering service.

They make wry faces at each other. As she goes up the
path to the HODSONS', DANIEL raises his voice at her.

DANIEL

You're welcome to them today.

LONDON AIRPORT. SUNDAY AFTERNOON.

BOB buys American magazines and walks to the Pan
Am counter.

132

ALEX'S STUDIO. SUNDAY AFTERNOON.

She comes in and finds an envelope with her name on it facing her on the floor, and a key like the one in her hand wrapped up in a piece of paper with a note:

COULD YOU LOOK AFTER THE TOUCAN FOR A BIT?

The TOUCAN stares at her from the window sill. She stares it out.

DANIEL'S CONSULTING ROOM. SUNDAY AFTERNOON.

DANIEL is in his patients' chair, with his back to camera. His own seat behind the desk is empty because he is managing a Hi-Fi nearer his grasp from this position. The Italian language-record is going.

RECORD

I prefer my scampi without garlic and my wife would like a steak if the meat is first class.

Record repeats phrase in Italian.

RECORD

Preferisco i miei scampi senz' aglio e mia moglie desidera una bistecca purchè la carne sia buonissima.

Pause for the student to repeat the Italian. DANIEL says the phrase, in a shorter time than the record allows. Pause.

Camera starts to move round very slowly. We see DANIEL's profile.

RECORD

You have used the present tense and the conditional. Now we will repeat the phrases in the past tense as if telling a story. "I said that I preferred

133

my scampi without garlic and my wife would have liked a steak provided that the meat was first class."

The record repeats the phrase in Italian. DANIEL speaks simultaneously with the record.

RECORD AND DANIEL

Ho detto che volevo i miei scampi senz' aglio e mia moglie avrebbe preferito la bistecca se la carne era buonissima.

RECORD

Molto bene. Arrivederci.

The gramophone switches itself off. By this time the camera movement has brought us to a view of DANIEL in full face, looking at the book on his knee. It is as if he is the patient now, talking to himself: or to us, it begins to be clear.

DANIEL

We went to hear "Aida" in the open air and it was not first class but we enjoyed the music and the landscape.

He repeats the phrase in Italian, lifting his head and staring straight at us.

DANIEL

Siamo andati a vedere l'Aida all'aria aperta. Saremmo andati a vedere l'Aida.
     (pause)
—Bugger the conditional.
     (pause)
When you're at school and want to quit, people say you're going to hate being out in the world. Well, I didn't believe them and I was right. When I was a kid I couldn't wait to be grown up and they said childhood was the best time of my life

134

and it wasn't. Now I want his company and people say, what's half a loaf, you're well shot of him; and I say, I know that, I miss him, that's all. They say he'd never have made me happy and I say, I am happy, apart from missing him. You might throw me a pill or two for my cough.

(pause)

All my life I've been looking for someone courageous and resourceful, not like myself, and he's not it.

(pause)

But something. We were something. You've no right to call me to account.

(pause)

I've only come about my cough.

He, too, stares us out.

Fade to black.

Full credits.